Passersthrough

Also by Peter Rock

Passersthrough

. . .

Peter Rock

Published by
Soho Press, Inc.
227 W 17th Street
New York, NY 10011

Library of Congress Cataloging-in-Publication Data
Names: Rock, Peter, author.
Title: Passersthrough / Peter Rock.
Description: New York, NY : Soho [2022]
Identifiers: LCCN 2021029616 |

ISBN 978-1-64129-343-3
eISBN 978-1-64129-344-0

Classification: LCC PS3568.O327 P37 20222
DDC 813'.54—dc21
LC record available at https://lccn.loc.gov/2021029616

Printed in the United States of America

10 9 8 7 6 5 4 3 2 1

Passersthrough

Helen: All you have to do is talk and it records what you say and then when I have time I can listen to it, no matter where I am, listen to what you tell me. Or I can read it—my computer or even my phone can transcribe what you say.

Benjamin: All these machines—I don't know. Is it really necessary?

H: For me, yes, I think so. It's necessary, for now, to talk to you.

B: All I want—

H: See how the green light comes on when it's recording? The orange light means it's standing by.

B: Waiting.

H: Yes.

B: Getting ready to listen.

H: You just have to be in range, close enough. I can put in our names, and then the software can even learn to recognize, identify our voices, the way we talk. It can even figure out punctuation, if it's working right. It can pause and wait, if there's a break. Be quiet for ten seconds and the light'll go orange, like it was before.

+

H: We can talk again.

B: Can we turn it off for a while? Just talk without it listening.

H: Forget about it. Look at me.

B: The light is green. It's listening.

H: Pretend it's not there. Don't look at it.

B: Can it see me?

H: Of course not.

B: This is silly. So far all it's recorded is a conversation about itself. I'm trying, Helen, I want so much to talk with you, to communicate. Can we talk about when you were a girl, and we used to go out in the forest together?

H: Let's take it slower; I have to go slow. Let's begin with some kind of introduction—I'd like to hear how you introduce yourself, actually.

B: But you know me.

H: Not really. Not for a long time.

B: Okay, then. Let's see. Typically, I breathe air, am omnivorous, and have eyes on the front of my head. I'm bipedal, often wear clothing and possess several skills. For instance, I'm handy with tools. The use of tools was once thought to differentiate man from animals, or the lower animals, yet scientists have witnessed primates with their straws and sticks, procuring ants from African anthills, and some experts believe that animals can cooperate with one another, even between species, without even being aware of it. There's a word for that relationship.

H: Why are you talking like an encyclopedia?

B: It's hard to be serious; this isn't exactly a conversation. And that word is "symbiotic."

H: Some facts about yourself, I meant. Start with your name.

B: My name is Benjamin Hanson. I'm seventy-six years old and my estranged daughter has installed machines in my house to facilitate our relationship. She believes I need a haircut, and is disappointed with many aspects of how I'm living my life. She won't discuss our past, and refuses to stay in my perfectly good guest room. She stays at a hotel, because her therapist has recommended that she not stay with me.

H: About yourself, not about me.

B: My name is Benjamin and I prefer to be called Benjamin. I wear sandals year-round. I was born in

September. This kind of thing? I prefer baths to showers, and suspenders to belts. I once owned a hardware store in Seattle, Washington, and before that I was born on Vancouver Island, yet my parents were Americans. I had many adventures there and later in Seattle had two children and a wife and then I had only one child and no wife and no hardware store. And so I moved to Portland, Oregon, to work for a time at Winks Hardware. I am now retired and continue to reside here in Portland, where I spend my days speaking clearly in the direction of a black plastic box with one piercing green eye.

H: I'm going to turn this off, now, to check and see that it's working.

+ + +

BENJAMIN LEANED BACK in his chair, watching as Helen tapped the switch on the front of the black machine. Its green light dimmed, then blinked out.

She walked across the room, nervously took her phone from her purse. Slender, she stood taller than he did, now—height was something that had drawn him to her mother, so long ago. Now the light from her phone illuminated her thin face, her sharp chin, her wide-set eyes. Was her hair always so dark? It was cut straight across, not quite touching her shoulders. She wore a black dress, her arms bare. Behind her, on the wall, hung a framed photo from long ago; in it, she had to be only two or three, laughing, wearing a stocking cap with round white buttons sewn on to look like eyes. She sat on Benjamin's shoulders, wore rubber boots (he remembered the feeling of those heels, kicking his chest), and her hands lay flat atop his head, where wispy hair still grew. He was laughing in the picture, his mouth wide open, all his teeth.

"What are you thinking about?" Helen said.

"Nothing."

"You're staring at me."

"Your mother must have taken that picture."

"What?" She turned to face the photograph. "Yes. That's a good one." After a moment, she looked back at him. "When was the last time you talked to her?"

"To your mother?" he said. "I don't know—it's strange. Ten years, almost? At least. More. I can't even remember what we talked about. And now I guess we won't talk again."

"I wondered if you might come to the funeral." Stepping closer, Helen held out her phone. On its screen he could see lines of words, too small to read.

"That's the transcription," she said, "the conversation we were just having."

He reached out his hand, but she'd already put the phone in her pocket. Stepping past him, brushing against his shoulder, she tapped the switch and the orange light blinked on again, turning green as they began to speak.

. . .

10/20/2018 2:57 PM Transcription of Audio Capture

B: What if I have nothing to say? To the machines, I mean. When you're not here, it'll be different.

H: That's the thing—I'll ask you questions with this bigger machine here.

B: The fax machine.

H: Yes, right. Every now and then, a page, a message from me will come out. I'll send you questions and then you can answer them by speaking. And if you have questions for me, you can speak them out loud and I'll receive them and answer. It'll be like a conversation.

B: We're having a conversation right now. A kind of conversation.

H: But we live in different places, and it's not always so easy to say things. For lots of reasons. I got you the computer, you know. Email—that's one way, but you won't even try—

B: Couldn't you just send me a letter?

H: I tried that. Twice. You never answered. You probably never opened them. Look at that pile of mail on the table, there. Remember how it was last month, before I put your bills on auto-pay? No electricity, no gas, no heat.

B: That always works itself out, eventually.

H: I mean, your driver's license is expired, your car registration—I hope you're not driving.

B: I can take care of myself. Couldn't we just talk on the phone?

H: We've talked about this, already. It's the same

problem—I can't just talk to you without stopping, without having time to process. It's not possible, not healthy.

B: We're talking, now. You seem fine to me.

H: How I seem to you and how I feel are different. And we are talking, but it's not easy. I'm trying, I'm trying to find a way where it's comfortable, where I can communicate with you. This is what I came up with, for now. Please don't touch my arm.

B: You act like you're afraid of me, and I'm just so happy to be with you again, together, and I feel like you're holding something against me that I don't even know what it is. If we can—

H: Just stop. You said, you agreed—

+

HELEN WALKED ACROSS the room, then. She opened the front door and stepped right through it without a word or any warning. The light on the machine blinked from green to orange.

Taking hold of his walking stick, Benjamin pulled himself to his feet and stood for a moment, finding his balance. He leaned over the table, the pile of mail—not one envelope from an actual person—and squinted through the window. Helen was walking away, her steps quick and angry. She didn't get into her rental car, but kept on past it, down the sidewalk.

The front door still open, Benjamin stepped out onto the porch. He could see Helen turning the corner at the end of the street, but he didn't follow, knew he couldn't catch her.

Next door, the neighbor boy, Javier, was coiling a long, green hose. Javier looked up, waved, then dragged the hose up the driveway, out of sight.

Benjamin stepped back inside his house, closed the door. He passed the unopened box, the computer Helen had sent him, then sat back down in his chair, facing the two machines, waiting for his daughter's return.

.   .   .

H: It was too much, it started feeling like it was
too much.

B: I'm sorry if I said something I shouldn't've said. But when you go like that, without saying anything, it feels like you might never come back.

H: You're being melodramatic. My flight's not for three hours, and I already told you I'd be back.

B: When?

H: A few weeks, next month? It depends on a lot of things.

+

B: You should say something about yourself.

H: What?

B: Like I did. Introduce yourself.

H: Fine. My name is Helen Hanson and I'm thirty-six years old and live in San Mateo, California, where I work for a software company, focused on issues of privacy and identity protection. My partner's name is Shauna. My father, I haven't been in touch with him for many years, but recently contacted him. This is my second visit since my mother's death. She died four months ago. I had a brother who passed away when he was seven and I was ten. Is that enough?

B: Maybe you could say why you contacted me, now, after all this time?

H: Well, okay. It probably was a lot of things, but when my mother died, in her things I found these envelopes, all addressed to me, eleven birthday cards from you to me—from my father, who my mother said was dangerous, who she said didn't want to be my father anymore. So that surprised me, that all those years maybe you were trying to reach me, and still wanted to be my father.

+ + +

HELEN SWITCHED OFF the machine again. Her eyes were closed, her hands on the arms of her chair as if she was about to stand.

"Tell me something you remember about me," Benjamin said. "Something from when you were a girl."

"Right now, I don't know—"

"Just one small thing, one untroubling thing."

Now Helen did stand. The wooden heels of her sandals rapped the floor as she left the room, disappeared into the kitchen. In a moment he heard the clatter of silverware, plates in the sink.

"I'm starting this dishwasher," she said. "Don't forget—it'll need to be unloaded, later on. And why's this camping stove on the counter?"

"Cleaning it."

"Where'd we put those scissors we bought? . . . Here, I found them. Let's do this outside."

Helen picked up a chair, and he followed her as she carried it out and across the yard, under the sequoia.

"This tree," she said. "It's more gigantic, up close."

Stepping out from the shadows, she set the chair in the middle of the grass. She unfolded the black polyester cape, snapping it around his neck as he sat down.

"I remember," she said, "one thing I remember is how you taught me to check to see if I was dreaming or awake. You told me to look closely at my hand, to see if it had the right number of fingers, if it looked like my hand? And then the jumping in the air to see if I'd float into the sky. Reading a sign and then looking away, looking back to see if the letters had changed. You told me all that."

"Yes," he said. "That sounds about right."

"Take off your glasses," she said, and he did, and the world around him went blurry. "Now," she said, running the comb down one side of his head, then the other, "how would you like it?"

"This was your idea," he said. "I think it's fine as it is."

"Like this? The bald-on-top-long-on-the-sides look? It's far from 'fine.'"

She began, the sharp metal sound next to his ear, the gentle tension as she combed, as she pulled at the hair on the back of his head, the release as she cut it away. Gray-and-white clumps of hair slid down the cape.

"You're getting along with the new neighbors all right?" she said.

"The neighbors?"

"Did you say you'd teach the boy to sharpen knives?"

"Yes, I did. Who told you that?"

"That worries people, that kind of thing."

"He seemed like he could use a friend, that boy, over there with only his mother."

"Do you befriend all the young boys in the neighbor-hood?"

"He's right next door. And I already taught him things, Javier. How to fix a toilet valve, rewire an outlet—"

Benjamin listened to the scissors, his daughter's breathing, the breeze high in the branches of the sequoia. Helen combed through snarls, she rested her free hand on his shoulder; she slapped at the hairs that clung to her black dress, she gently leaned against him. He wished he had more hair, that this process could last much longer than it would.

"You know what I'd like?" he said. "I'd like to go on a hike together, up in the mountains. We could camp, even, like we used to do. Our misadventures—isn't that what we called them?"

"I don't want to talk about this. This is exactly what I don't want to talk about."

"We won't get lost—"

"Hold still." Her hand on his shoulder, the top of his head.

"Sad Clown Lake," he said. "Can we talk about Sad Clown Lake?"

"Not right now, we can't." Helen stepped back, took out her phone, checked the time. "Now I really do have to get going."

"You came back after all these years and we can't talk about what happened?"

"Not now. I can't, not yet. Should I trim your eyebrows?"

She stepped back, bent down to his level, stared at him. "Yes, I should."

She lay the comb over one eye, snipped across. Then the other eye.

"Better," she said. "Much better."

Unsnapping the polyester cape from his neck, she swung it sharply through the air, black against the gray sky.

The next morning, birdsong in the yard, then the rough capering of the squirrels along the top of the fence, just outside Benjamin's window.

And then another sound, a scratching sound, from the living room. A mouse? A beep, a hum. No, it was the machine, the paper pulled through the fax machine in the living room.

Slowly swinging his bony legs around, he set his bare feet on the wooden floor, snatched his jeans from the bedpost and untwisted their suspenders, found a clean shirt. New white socks, Velcro tightened on his sandals. He lifted his eyeglasses from the bedside table, stood, and ran his hand along the wall as he stepped to the door, into the living room.

The paper was still warm when he took it from the machine's tray.

Facsimile

TO B	FROM Helen
COMPANY	COMPANY
FAX (503) 517-7659	FAX (650) 234-2920
SUBJECT	DATE 10.21.2018 8:47 AM

Hello. I've been thinking of you, since my visit. I'm not
sure if this is a better way, but we can try.

I need you to understand that I really don't remember
everything that happened, when I was a girl. To think
about that whole period of time isn't easy for me. The
things I do remember, I was told they were impossible,
that they didn't happen, that they were covering up something more painful, traumatic, something you did to me.

It's true that we called those times in the forest our misadventures—that was our funny name for it, and it was funny,
until something actually went wrong, and then the word "misadventure" really meant misadventure again. So it doesn't feel
like a word we can joke about or use in that way anymore.

I don't want to sound like I'm accusing you.

Finding those birthday cards was so surprising, par-
tially because of the fact that Mom had opened them—read

them, I guess—and then hadn't thrown them away, had kept them all together like she might give them to me, someday. Which I guess she kind of did? The cards are so cheesy, all hippos and dogs and balloons, like you never seemed to understand that I was older than when you last saw me, like I wasn't growing up. You always sign off *Daddy*, and you write almost nothing, maybe reminding me of Derek, telling me not to forget something about him, like the way he called squirrels "quirls" or how you used to make up songs to sing to me and him.

I'm writing from my office—I need to get to work. You probably don't understand what I do every day, but maybe you'd find it interesting, to know what I've grown up to do. Mostly I am writing code, which is computer language, to keep people from accessing other people's information— so they can't impersonate you, steal your identity. I'm making up systems like passwords or encryptions or other kinds of authentication to fool automated attacks. I'll have a person click on every box in a grid that shows a street sign, or a motorcycle. Am I even making sense to you?

The danger is that some malicious person will gain access to your private information and then be able to convince other people that they're you.

I remember how you would make me eat the wild plants, and how you would pull back the tall grass and weeds along the house, and that one time you picked those termites off the wall and ate them, and tried to make me eat one.

You left me out in the woods with only a compass, then took the compass away, to see if I could get back on my own. I remember you blindfolding me, which was part of the game. Did you tie a rope to me, and follow?

We used to cross out the names of everything on the map, when we were out in the wilderness, and make up our own names, write them in.

Sad Clown Lake. Was that a real place? Was there a lake? Or was it only the game we played, that went wrong?

End

BENJAMIN SET THE pages on the kitchen counter, then opened the refrigerator: the protein shakes, the cheese and vegetables that Helen had bought him at Trader Joe's the day before. He took out an apple, filled a glass with water. Pouring in a coffee packet, he swirled his finger through the water, then drank the bitter mixture down.

In the living room, he switched on the machine; the orange light grew brighter, waiting. He stood there, uncertain what to say, unable to begin.

. . .

OUTSIDE, WIND RUSHED through the sequoia's branches, but the rain was holding off. He locked the back door, put his keys in his pocket, checked the money there, rolled in its rubber band. Walking stick in hand, he headed down the driveway.

It was late enough now that Bi-Mart was open, that he could purchase fuel for the camping stove, perhaps investigate the things they'd need, if he convinced Helen to come camping. New sleeping bags, good ones, for both of them. A folding saw. Of course a blue tarp.

"Move!"

Halfway across the street, he was almost hit by a bicyclist— it was a teenager in a bright orange cap, one hand holding a second, riderless bicycle by the handlebars, coasting alongside. The pedals of this second bicycle turned, jerking around and around with no feet pushing them.

Past the coffee shop, past the Safeway, the dry cleaners.

Benjamin caught his breath, continued toward Bi-Mart. The parking lot was almost empty, abandoned metal carts glinting in the sun. He passed stacked bags of bark chips and compost, potting soil, headed around an old red Chevy pickup with a dented aluminum camper on the back that was parked between him and the entrance.

The camper was tall, a full-sized door on its back, pasted with a sticker that read NO SOLICITING. Down lower, on the bumper: WOOD IS GOOD and TIMBERS and FARMED SALMON DYED FOR YOU.

The aluminum camper was warm against his fingers; he leaned, walked alongside it. Just as he reached the truck's cab, a kind of strangled cough rose up, close.

And then a sharpness struck his face and everything was suddenly, searingly gone.

.   .   .

WHEN HE OPENED his eyes, he was flat on his back, on the pavement next to the truck. He could hardly see. There was a scrabbling, a shouting, footsteps coming closer.

A girl leaned over him. A dark stone, dangling by a cord from her neck, swung close to his face.

"You okay? You're okay."

She glanced around at the crowd gathering.

"He's all right," she said. "I know him. Just give him room to breathe."

As she spoke, he realized that she was a woman, not a girl. Her voice low, gravelly, she was telling people what was going to happen, that she had the situation under control. He tried to sit up, and blood slid into his eyes. The woman reached out, dabbed at his face with something in her hand. Somewhere a dog was barking; the sound echoed as if caught in a distant cave.

"You're taking him to the hospital?" another voice said. "Did someone call someone?"

"Yes," the woman said. "It's fine, everything's fine. I know him."

"I'd just like to go home," Benjamin said. "If I can get to my feet."

"Everyone, back *up*," she said, then to him again, her voice lower. "Is this your cane, here? You can see, can't you?"

"My glasses," he said.

"Ah." She leaned over him, stretching an arm beneath the truck. "Here. I'll hold on to these." Standing, she opened the truck's passenger door and in a moment was tying a piece of fabric around his head. "You can stand, now? Here, lean on me. Just pivot, here, into the truck. Up. There you go."

He was sitting in her truck now. She slammed the door,

and he could see the dim shape of her running around the front, the driver's door opening, the engine cranking and catching. As they pulled away, in the rearview mirror he could see the blurry figures of the people who had been gathered around him.

"Spectators," the woman said. "Was anyone taking pictures, do you think?"

"What?" Benjamin said.

"With their phones." She turned right, accelerating away from the parking lot.

"Can I have my glasses?"

"They're broken."

"I don't need a hospital," he said. "I don't think—"

"No way we're going to a hospital," she said. "I'll pull over in a minute here; I have some things in the back where I can fix you up."

"Would you please just take me home?"

His head felt hollow, all pain and surface, the blood drying on his face. He still heard the dog barking, as if it were in his head, or chasing them.

"We're going the wrong way, I think."

"What?"

"I live in the opposite direction," he said.

"Alone?"

"Go out to Fifty-Second, then go left at the light."

"You live alone?"

"Yes."

The woman swung the truck around; a blurry parked car rose up alongside, a near collision. Again, the sound of the dog barking. They climbed the steep hill of Woodstock, the truck lurching through the intersection as the light turned from yellow to red.

Voices shouted as they passed the Bi-Mart parking lot again.

"Already, this day," she said.

His left eye was working better than the right. Long, jagged cracks divided the windshield. He squinted across the cab: the woman wore a sweatshirt and tan overalls, cut off at the knee. Was she barefoot? A flat piece of metal shaped like a machete slid around beneath her feet. His vision blurred again.

"Is a dog chasing us?" he said.

"He's in the back," she said. "You startled him—otherwise he'd never have bitten you."

"What?"

"It's fine," she said. "Totally fine, now. I turn here?"

"Yes, and then right."

"And no one's home?"

"I don't know you," he said.

"I know that."

"You said you knew me."

"My name's Melissa," she said. "What's the house number?"

"The blue one. Is it coming up?"

"I'll just pull past a little bit." She parked and switched off the ignition, keys in her hand. "Wait here."

Opening her door, she leapt out, disappeared around the back of the truck.

Benjamin sat there for a moment, then opened his own door. His right eye was stuck shut, but he adjusted the cloth on his head so he could see, blurrily, from his left. He shifted around, slid his feet down to the pavement.

"What are you doing?" Melissa said, leaning out from behind the truck. "Did I ask you to stay put? Now, come here."

She was unlocking the back door of the camper; inside, the barking got louder, turned to whining.

Stepping on the bumper, she climbed up, opening the door just enough to slip inside; a black, graying snout, a flash of teeth stuck through the gap, and then the snarling and whining subsided as the door slammed closed again.

Benjamin stood there, waiting. Looking down, he realized that the front of his shirt, his socks were bright red with blood. Pain shifted along his skull as he tilted his head.

The camper door opened, and Melissa climbed down.

In one hand, a small canvas bag; in the other, a red plastic box like a tackle box. Benjamin squinted past her, into the camper; the dog—a hazy black shape, was now at the far end—tied there?—near a small ledge that looked like a bed. There was a blurry kitchen and, closer, a table.

"You live in there?" he said.

"Sometimes." She closed the door, locked it. "Lean on me. Here. Wait, did you have a cane? Wait." She rushed to the cab of the truck, returned with his stick. "Now, let's take it slow. No one's inside? The back door would be better. There is a back door, right? Can we go around? Great. Yes, here, down the driveway."

He was so tired, all at once. Exhausted. He leaned against Melissa, her head barely reaching his shoulder. Her hair brushed his face—stiff, curly and dark, pulled back, bleached lighter at the tips. He struggled with the keys, led her into the kitchen, listened as she washed her hands at the sink.

"Where we going, here?" she said, but she didn't wait.

He trailed her, into the living room, through it. She moved so quickly.

"Don't worry about the blood," she said. "I'll clean that up, later. Can you sit down? Here, this is your bedroom? Good. No, wait. The bathroom's better."

She sat Benjamin down on the edge of the tub, then

opened the plastic box, took glass jars from the canvas bag, lined them up on the tile counter. He felt a jerk at one foot, then the other, the sound of Velcro, then his bloody socks pulled off, thrown aside. Next, a click, the glint of a knife's blade, a pull at the neck of his shirt; cold metal at his neck, and then she cut the shirt away.

"Can you stand?" Melissa unbuckled her overalls, pulled off her sweatshirt—she wore a white, ribbed tank top underneath—and threw it out the door, onto his bed. "Very good," she said, buckling the straps of her overalls again. "Now, take off your pants."

"I'm home," he said. "That's all I wanted. You can leave me."

"You're still disoriented," she said. "I'd feel responsible if that bite got infected. And I want to take a look at your eye, too. How's your vision?"

"Not great," he said. "You still have my glasses?"

"They broke, remember?"

Melissa left the room; in a moment, he could hear her opening and closing the drawers of his dresser. When she returned, she was tearing something—one of his T-shirts—into strips.

"What's your name?" she said.

"Benjamin."

Now she was soaking strips of the fabric in the sink,

pouring in a plastic bottle of rubbing alcohol. She began wiping down his neck, his hands.

"That dog," he said.

"You're shivering, Ben." Melissa pulled a towel from the rack, draped it over his shoulders. "You startled him, suddenly appearing like that. You can't blame him. He was sitting in the truck and then there, there was your face. It surprised him." She unwound the wrapping from his head; it was a pale blue dress shirt, dark with blood. She dropped it onto the floor. "Some of this is going to sting, Ben."

"Benjamin."

"That's too much name for me right now. You're not going to shout or scream?"

"I don't think so."

She leaned close—sweat and vanilla in his nose, and he felt the warmth of her skin, her mouth slightly open, her breath whistling through a gap where she was missing a bottom tooth. Her dark eyes were intent and her hands gentle, dabbing away at the blood, taking up a clean strip of cloth.

"It's not so bad," she said. "Mostly blood. Here, try to open your eye. Looks good. Just the puncture wounds—I'm kind of impressed, Johnson getting old the way he is, those teeth."

"Who?"

"The dog," she said, leaning closer again. "Now, this'll definitely sting."

There was a tattoo—two black X's—behind her ear, the dark gray stone on a leather thong around her neck, a twist of black string at her wrist. A stripe of his blood marked the skin of her upper arm, and her skin was darker than his, contrasting with his pale white legs, the hair all fallen out, the varicose veins on his calves.

"Now let's see if that'll dry a little," she said. "Sit still."

Benjamin watched as she rose up from where she'd been crouching; she took some green leaves from the canvas bag, put them in her mouth, and began to chew.

"Do you still have my glasses?"

Melissa tore strips of white tape, sticking them along the counter, a row of tongues. Leaning forward, then, she suddenly spat a green paste into one of the glass jars.

"This," she said. "I'll put this poultice on you now, but then you should clean and replace it twice a day until this jar is empty. I'll make up some more before I go."

She slapped the green mixture, cold and sticky, on his face; he felt it gradually drying, hardening.

"We should get you resting." She snatched the strips of tape up one by one as she secured gauze over the wound. "You own this place? Or you rent it?"

"It's my house, yes."

"Any relatives nearby?"

"No. My daughter, she's in California."

"You can stand? Here, easy. Maybe you could lie down in bed? I got the blanket, there. Yes, very good. Here, prop your head higher. You rest while I clean a few things up."

Flat on his back, he stared at the familiar cracks forking across the ceiling, then closed his eyes. He heard voices outside, cars driving up and down the street. Inside the house, he could hear Melissa going room to room, opening drawers and doors and cabinets.

"Close your eyes. Rest."

She reappeared, a plastic bag in her hand; snatching his bloody clothes from the floor, she jammed them into the bag, then began to clean the bathroom. Once she was done, she dragged the bag behind her, waving to Benjamin as she passed the bed.

A slithering sound, fainter and fainter, moving through the house.

The front door opened, closed.

Silence.

The phone was ringing. Benjamin tried to sit up; a wave of pain echoed in his face. The ringing continued. After a moment, he rolled from his bed and slowly crawled through the living room, to the kitchen.

When he lifted the headset from its cradle on the wall, he lost hold and it bounced away, a small voice saying "hello" as he dragged it back by the cord.

"Hello?" he said.

"Are you okay?"

"Who is this? Helen?"

"What happened?" she said. "I got a message—just a scrap, someone else's voice saying not to worry about the blood, that they'd clean it up."

"What?"

"From a couple hours ago, from the machine. I think it was a woman's voice?"

"I had an accident," he said. "I had a small accident and a friend came over to help me bandage it."

"What friend?"

"A woman I met. It was her dog."

"Her dog what?"

"It was a dog bite, what happened."

"And you let her in the house?"

"It's my house," he said. "I'm fine. It's nothing."

"I was—I was just surprised that it wasn't your voice, and then the blood. I was worried about you; I am worried."

"Thank you," he said. "Thank you for worrying, but I didn't know you were listening like that."

Leaning forward, Benjamin stretched his free hand and pulled the paper from the counter, the fax she'd sent, all about the termites and the compass and the map with the crossed-out names. He could barely make out the words.

"I guess," she said, "I guess you could turn the machine off, unless you want it to record."

"Don't you feel," he said, "whatever people say, don't you know that I would never have hurt you?"

"I didn't—"

"What you remember," he said, "that doesn't have to be covering up something you don't remember. It could just be what happened."

Taking hold of the counter's edge, he pulled himself to his feet. A blurry shape, next to the toaster—his glasses, missing one temple, the left lens cracked and the right one gone altogether. He held them to his face, closed his right eye. The sequoia's green branches waved through the window. A basketball rose above the top of the fence— appearing, disappearing—as the neighbor boy, unseen, threw it up in the air.

"I think—" Helen's voice was halting, choked down, when she finally spoke. "I still think it's best if we only talk on the phone if it's an emergency."

10/21/2018 8:22 PM Transcription of Audio Capture

Benjamin: Helen, hello. Thank you for the phone call, earlier. Thanks for worrying about me.

+

Someone walking by outside might wonder about me in here, all alone, talking and waving my hands in the air. I'm waving my hands at these machines while I talk to them, to you. Helen, hello.

+

When you were a little girl, maybe I didn't ask to go to the forest? I just said, and then we did. Out around Mount Rainier and you'd run ahead, torn-up flowers in your hands, and I, I was teaching you the names of things. I had the feeling that I could walk forever with you there ahead, or trailing, or off to the side invisible in the bushes.

+

Sometimes I think or dream of your mother being there, too, how that would be, and even your little brother, the four of us.

+

The other day I saw a small red mitten, stuck on a fence post like it was waving at me, all the way down the street as I walked closer. Some child had lost it, someone had put it there. When I saw it I began to cry. Even now I see all these signs, I see them as messages from Derek.

+

When we were talking before I called you my estranged daughter and since then it's been bothering me, whether that was the right word or I was angry or what. That word "estranged"–do you think it means that things between people who were once close become, get caught in a situation where they're like strangers?

+

I have so much to say, and questions, and you've said you're fragile and I don't want to drive you away. What I would've liked to ask you, when you were here, was for a hug, but for some reason when you are actually here that's an awkward, impossible kind of question for me to ask you.

+

Anyway, out there I remember the blue sky and how the trees swayed. Even if you didn't feel the way I felt you must've felt some way. Now you're grown but you can't have forgotten all we did. I'm still your father. Now I'm older but I haven't forgotten the blue tarp, the lean-to, Sad Clown Lake.

+

Why can't you at least tell me what you remember? I'll believe you, even if other people haven't.

+

Breakfast. Benjamin stood in the kitchen, drinking his cold, grainy coffee. His face, his whole head hurt, the gauze stiff around the edges, slipping down over his eye. He picked up a granola bar, tore the wrapper open, and took a bite, but that was too painful; he put the bar away in his pocket, steadied the glasses on his face.

Across the backyard, his tree, his sequoia rose up, holding back the sun. And then, in its shadow, movement. A body. A boy, outside, standing in the yard. Javier.

Benjamin found his walking stick, opened the door.

Javier looked up, his dark eyes wide, his black hair ragged. "What happened to you?" he said. "Your face . . ."

Benjamin was easing down the steps; it was difficult, as he had no depth perception, one eye closed. He adjusted his glasses, sending another wave of pain across his skull.

"It's fine, my friend. It's nothing." Reaching into his

pocket, he held out the granola bar. "Here. It's chocolate chip."

Javier grasped the bar, looked it over, took a bite.

"I know, the knife sharpening," Benjamin said. "That'll have to wait, I'm afraid."

"It's something else," the boy said. "I saw someone, that's why I came over. Someone, someone was in your tree. A boy—older than me, but a boy, and he climbed up there and he left something."

Benjamin squinted across the yard, closing his right eye. He walked over under the tree, where a canvas bag hung from a low branch. Reaching up, he unhooked it.

"I was going to give it to you," Javier said. "I was going to get it for you."

And then, suddenly, there were two men in green uniforms, walking up the driveway and standing at the edge of the yard. The crack in Benjamin's eyeglasses made it seem as if they stood crookedly, their legs attached at an angle.

"Sir?" one said to him. "Are you okay?"

"Who are you?"

"Your face . . ."

"It's healing," Benjamin said. "I'm fine."

"We're here to work on your yard today, if that's okay with you."

"Pardon me?"

"Your daughter set it up," the man said. "She said to tell you not to worry."

The boy had already hurried away, down the driveway, as the man spoke. The other man was unloading their equipment from the truck.

. . .

BENJAMIN UNZIPPED THE canvas bag and turned it over, spilled its contents across the kitchen table.

His keys, his roll of cash held tight with the rubber band, a pair of new red suspenders. Three separate pairs of eyeglasses that he hadn't seen before, all made of heavy, black plastic. Last, a white envelope, its seams unsealed, flattened out. It appeared to have been sent from a collection agency, and was addressed to Beverly Anderson at 7734 SE 66th Avenue; on the other side, what had been the inside, a note had been written.

Ben,

Sorry about your clothes. Here are the rest of the things. You remember what I said about washing your face and reapplying the poultice? I hope it's not swelling. Please don't contact anyone about the incident. I'll try to come check on you soon. I couldn't get the blood out of your socks or pants.

M

IN THE BATHROOM, he started to pull at the white tape, to loosen the bandage, but it was too much. He took a breath, gripped one edge of the tape, then tore it off at once—the pain doubled him over, his forehead just missing the tile of the counter. The pain reverberated through his skull, only slowly dissipated.

Outside, the roar of the mower, the leaf blower, the men's heads going back and forth across the bedroom window. Benjamin closed the bathroom door.

Warm water broke down the crust, the brown blood gone red down the sink. In the mirror he could see the four deep teeth marks in his forehead, his temple, black. They were no longer bleeding, but the skin around them ran from purplish black to lighter blue.

He opened the jar, smelled the green mixture—seaweed? The liquid had separated, and so he put the top back on and shook, to mix it up again. Carefully, he lay out the gauze, the strips of white tape as Melissa had done. He slapped the green mixture on the skin of his face.

Facsimile

TO B	FROM Helen
COMPANY	COMPANY
FAX (503) 517-7659	FAX (650) 234-2920
SUBJECT	DATE 10.22.2018 1:04 PM

After all this time, to hear your voice coming out of the tiny speaker on my phone, or to read the lines and lines of little words that you've said, sitting there in your living room, waving your arms, it's uncomfortable because I haven't been allowed to or even let myself think of you or of that time and I want to be curious, to be generous, but I can't help that I'm angry, that anger rises up. That might be because of what you did, or why, and it might be that it's not your fault.

It's frustrating. You're frustrating, but I want to understand, to forgive you even if that word upsets you or doesn't quite fit. I do think writing helps, and I can write things I couldn't say to you, and I can read or hear things from a distance that would be harder to listen to up close.

I remember the straw hat you always wore, on those days we went into the forest. I can see how your hands looked,

when they were teaching my hands, when you were teaching
me to tie knots, when they were tying the knots that
attached the blue tarp to the frame of the lean-to. And
now you say that was at Sad Clown Lake? Sometimes I think
I can remember that lake. Was it shallow? And so cold. We
could see bones, white bones that you said were probably
the bones of deer, just below the surface.

I do remember that I was looking for a place, I thought
we might find Derek, somehow, that I might talk to him
even though he was dead. And you, you encouraged me,
which is something I don't understand, that you let me
do, let me believe that we might find him.

I started writing this last night and then I had to go to
sleep and so I'll finish it now, during my lunch break.
You keep asking, and now I'm afraid you'll be disappointed if I tell you what I actually remember, because
it isn't that much, and it feels so incomplete.

Mom always talked about you in the past tense, as someone
from our past, unreachable, and she talked about that
time in the forest as something I survived. I came out
the other side, she said, so dwelling on it wasn't
going to help me when what she wanted was for me to pay

attention to the present and especially the future.
I know I got lost out there, but was it that you lost
track of me, or that I was running from you?

One troubling part is that when I think about all we did
in the forest, when I remember, I'm happy.

End

The next afternoon, the wind rustled in the trees overhead, and the sun shone bright in the muddy puddles along the sidewalk. Benjamin counted up the numbered avenues as he walked. Sixty-Fourth, Sixty-Fifth. The other day, driving to Trader Joe's, Helen had called this neighborhood "Felony Flats"; that name wasn't used by people who lived here.

Two cats—one tabby, one black—stood on the back of a couch, behind a picture window; they swiveled their heads in unison, watching him pass. He pulled out the envelope, checked the address again. *7734 SE 66th Ave.* When he took a left on Sixty-Sixth, he saw Melissa's red truck, halfway down the block. Parked on the dirt beside the street, its camper topper reflecting the sun.

Cautiously, he approached. He felt as if he were being observed, but he couldn't see anyone. Stretching out his walking stick, he rapped on the truck's metal bumper, below the rectangular door of the camper, then stepped back; he waited for the dog's bark, for the door to suddenly jerk open.

Silence.

Stepping closer, he reached out. The knob turned in his hand, and he pulled it outward, squinted inside. A sleeping bag, in the bed above the cab. Pieces of electronics, computer parts strewn along the floor. A hammer on the chair, atop an unfolded map; on the table, insulated plastic coffee cups, pliers, a tangle of wire.

"Looking for Melissa?"

Benjamin leapt back, almost falling, the door slapping shut, his stick clattering on the ground.

It was only a boy, a teenager astride a bike; reddish hair, thick freckles on his face. He wore bright yellow rubber gloves, gripping the handlebars of a bike that had been painted completely white, decorated with plastic flowers. Blue and pink and orange and red.

"You're the old guy Johnson bit?" The boy squinted. "Obviously! Your face is a freaking wreck! I been to your house, that big tree and everything! That was like a secret mission I was on. Mission accomplished."

"Where's Melissa?" Benjamin said.

"Not out here, boss." The boy started down the street. "Follow me." Climbing off the bike, he pushed it along through the puddles, the sparse gravel. There was no side-walk, here. When the boy looked back, Benjamin stopped.

"Stop acting so afraid!" The boy laughed. "You afraid of me? You should be."

They walked again. Several houses down from where the truck was parked, the boy wheeled the bike through a rickety gate, toward a small, weather-beaten bungalow. Blackberry vines climbed all the way up one side; the roof sagged, as if it might collapse under their weight.

"Not the front door. This way."

As the boy disappeared around the side of the house, suddenly a voice rose up—Benjamin recognized it as Melissa's:

"Cisco! Take that right back wherever you found it."

"What? Why?" the boy said. "It wasn't even locked up. I know—I can paint it, I'll have to, but everything works. Pump up the tires, oil the chain a little. Someone'll totally buy it."

Benjamin hung back, listening, out of view.

"That's a ghost bike," Melissa said.

"A what?"

"That's a dead person's bike. Someone died, probably hit by a car, and so their friends set up that bike to remember the spot. You can't steal a ghost bike—that's the worst kind of bad luck."

"But I could paint it—"

"Did you hear me?" she said.

Benjamin leaned out slightly, squinting into the yard. Melissa was facing sideways, her hands on her hips; she seemed to be daring the boy to keep arguing his point. Her hair was loose, a tangle of black and yellow curls, and she wore the same cutoff overalls as the day before, her dark arms bare. She still wore no shoes.

"What about this house, being in this house?" the boy said. "You acting like you're worried about dead people, now?"

"We're not disrespecting anyone," she said. "That bike, don't even get it close to me—that's like a curse."

"Whatever," the boy said. "Anyway, this old dude's come looking for you."

She looked up, past the boy as he turned the bike around, and the tone of her voice shifted.

"Well, Ben! Isn't this a surprise! Didn't I say I'd come check on you?"

"I was just walking." Benjamin held up the note she'd left, the flattened envelope, and gestured at the address on the other side. "I'm sorry—"

"Don't be sorry. Maybe I wanted you to find me." She stepped closer, touched his shoulder. "Maybe it's really not a surprise at all."

The boy began shouting, now, from out in the street:

"It's a freaking totally good bike!" He gestured as if he were throwing something with both gloved hands, then pedaled away down the block.

"He your son?" Benjamin said.

"What?" Melissa laughed. "Cisco—no, he's my little brother, like a brother."

"Why's he wearing those gloves?"

"Something to do with his hands?" she said. "I have no idea. Here, come inside."

She opened the door and led him through a half-demolished kitchen, around a hole in the floor so he wouldn't fall through; he glimpsed the shadowy concrete of the basement, below.

"You live here?"

"People share it."

They stopped in a square room that must have once been a bedroom. Another door, on the far wall, and one window, solid green: dense blackberry vines with their leaves and thorns pressed against the glass. The window was open just enough for a thick orange extension cord to snake in, next to a round black cable and a thinner cord, attached with alligator clips to a pale yellow rotary telephone. Next to the phone, on the floor, two televisions—no, computer monitors—were plugged into the orange cord, casting flickering light along the wall.

Melissa stepped over the cords, to the window; she stared at the green vines as if she could see through them.

"I see one of those pairs of glasses worked out okay?"

"Seems to." He reached up, touched the frames.

"You didn't mention it to anyone," she said, "what happened, the other day?"

"No," he said.

"I was thinking," she said, "that maybe we might go on a hike together, the two of us, out in the forest."

"A hike?"

"I thought you liked that kind of thing. A misadventure."

"A what? Why'd you use that word?"

"Because I read the message your daughter sent." Melissa smiled, and her tongue showed, sharp in the gap between her teeth. "That fax, at your house. What? Why are you making that face?"

"Those weren't for you to read," he said.

"Whatever," she said. "Here—" She pulled a chair into the center of the room. "Let's have a look at your face."

When she motioned for him to come closer, at first he thought she wanted him to sit down; instead, she stood on the chair and leaned over, into him, her soft breast against his shoulder, the warmth of her body, the scent of dirt and vanilla. She took off his glasses, handed them to him.

"Tilt your head back." Slowly, she pulled at the bandage, brought her face close. "You sure look better than the last time I saw you."

"I did what you told me," he said, "with that mixture."

"A cat bite's worse than a dog's, and human's the worst, for infection." She was pushing the tape back against his skin. "This looks pretty good, actually."

Hopping down from the chair, she stepped across to a white dresser that had one corner propped up with a phone book, four plastic jugs of water lined atop it. She picked one up, removed the top and took a long drink, then held it out to him.

"So," she said, "you left your daughter out in the woods with a compass, and she got lost?"

"It wasn't like that."

"What was it like? You blindfolded her?"

"It's hard to explain."

"I guess so. Seems like it was a little confusing."

The phone on the floor began to ring, echoing suddenly in the room, and Melissa bent down, snatched up the handset.

"Hello? Okay, wait. Hold on." Covering the mouthpiece, she turned to Benjamin. "This'll take a minute." She carefully stretched the phone's cord along the floor, went through the door, and closed it behind her.

Benjamin could hear her voice, but couldn't tell what she

was saying, only that she sounded agitated, as if something was not going as expected. The jug of water was heavy in his hand; he returned it to the dresser; he noticed a blue yoga mat, standing rolled up against the wall, a collection of crinkled-up aluminum foil in the corner.

The door opened behind him, and Melissa returned, hung up the phone, then pushed it against the wall with her foot.

"Tomorrow," she said. "Or, no, the day after tomorrow. We hike."

"I never said I was going somewhere with you."

"I'll bring everything we need," she said. "I'll pick you up close to noon. Right now, though, I'm already late."

With that, she brushed past him, waving as she hurried back out through the kitchen.

Benjamin looked once more around the room, in the silence. He stepped close to the wall, where he could see the computer screens: one showed a street scene, a car driving by; on the other, colored lines bounced back and forth, making designs. It shifted, then—a figure coasted by on a skateboard. One direction, then the other. In a moment, the same figure, bouncing a ball along the sidewalk. A car slid down the street, was engulfed in static, surfaced again.

Turning, he went through the door, followed the way Melissa had gone. In the kitchen, carefully stepping around the hole in the floor, he glimpsed movement, down below, something in the darkness of the basement. Shifting shadows, a body moving slowly from side to side. The sound of scraping, or something smoother, rhythmic.

"Hello?" he said.

The black dog lifted its head, then, and looked up at him, its eyes glinting before it barked once, bent down again, and resumed licking at the concrete floor.

By the time Benjamin reached the front yard, Melissa and her truck were nowhere to be seen.

10/22/2018   5:17 PM   Transcription of Audio Capture

Benjamin: If when you remember our time together
in the forest, you feel happy, that should tell you
something.

+

You were blindfolded and you were barefoot or in
your moccasins and you led me deep into the forest.
A house, you said, you wanted to have a house,
there where no one could find it. That's why the
lean-to, the blue tarp, everything that followed.
You kept adding things—the stove, the food, the
notebook, and I followed, I was following because
you seemed to already know, to have an idea, a connection to something impossible because you were
so young that you could still see things to try.

+

Remember that I was the one who called, who reported
you missing. If I did something wrong, why would
I have called? Another thing is that sleeping out
there alone was something you wanted to do. It

wasn't something I suggested. And Derek—I don't really remember it that way, like I thought we could find him. I knew we missed him, talked about him, but I just wanted us to do something special together, the two of us.

+

I woke up and checked for you in the lean-to, under the blue tarp, and you weren't there, and the lean-to wasn't there. Everything was gone. That's all I know. You were gone in the night, and I looked everywhere, and searched, and I couldn't find you.

+

I thought I knew what I wanted to say. I speak into this machine and the words go out of me and I can't change them, can't double-check them.

+

All these years you've listened to your mother, which is fine, but I don't even know what she said.

I don't know what you said, for that matter, what was your recollection, what you told her and what you told them, the counselors or the police. They didn't let me talk to you and I know you felt, you feel that I somehow gave up on you when I moved and lost touch and in a way, okay, but they threatened me and I couldn't talk to you. Child endangerment, they said. There was no way I could convince anyone, no talking that would make things better and not worse. So I went away.

+

I remember how once you hid in a pile of leaves and let me walk on by, how I thought I'd lost you and I screamed myself hoarse before you leapt out, laughing. How soft, how small your hand was, in mine, walking under the trees.

+

Yes, we did cross out the names on the map and write in our own names, mostly made up by you. Did I tie a rope to you? I can't remember that but you could be right, I didn't want to lose you—terrible to say it, I know, considering that you did get lost, that I did lose you.

+

You were blindfolded, that was part of it. And you'd take off your boots and go barefoot or put on your moccasins. It was, I don't know how much I explained, back then, or how much you could understand why we were doing what we were doing or if you could remember it, now. Which is why I need you to tell me how you remember it. I only had you so few days, every other weekend, and I wanted to find something, an activity, a place that was for just the two of us, that was secret.

+

I believed, I think I thought that a child, if I blindfolded you, especially, because of innocence or intuition, you'd be a better guide at finding that place, at wandering us into it. I'd follow.

+

So. So that's a way to get to, to talk about Sad Clown Lake, a lake you led us to. It was a lake, sometimes, and sometimes it wasn't a lake. You named it. That's where we built our lean-to, which was sometimes next to the lake, that could only be found by getting lost, that was never in the same place twice. The wooden stakes and later the stove, everything, the slanted roof and the blue tarp. The two of us! The sound of the wind under that blue tarp made it sound like a sail, like the two of us were sailing together, and we were.

+

We were going somewhere that no one had ever been.

+

Benjamin: Looking around, last night, I found this old article and maybe you have it or have seen it, I don't know. Maybe it'll help? I'm going to try to figure out how to fax it with this machine.

+

Facsimile

TO	FROM
COMPANY	COMPANY
FAX (650) 234-2920	FAX (503) 517-7659
SUBJECT	DATE 10.23.2018 8:03 AM

Lost Girl Found
Seattle Times
September 15, 1993
by Sabrina Hong

Helen Hanson, 11, has been found, almost a week after she went missing in the wilderness of Mount Rainier National Park. On Tuesday, local authorities were contacted by Ronald and Celeste Nordhaus of Klickitat. The girl had walked out of the trees near their remote farmhouse and appeared to be unharmed, though shaken.

Klickitat farmhouse where Hanson was recovered.

Law enforcement, volunteers and Wilderness First Responders had combed the area where the girl first went missing. One unexplained detail is how Hanson was found over a hundred miles from where her father claimed she was last seen.

Initial reports were unclear whether the father and daughter were hiking, or camping overnight. While the father, Benjamin Hanson, 51, continues to be questioned with regard to the incident, he did not respond to multiple requests for an interview. Employees at the Ballard Ace Hardware Store that Hanson owns reported that he had been working sporadically this week, as he was largely involved in the search for his daughter.

Helen was released to the care of her mother, Eliese Kitson, 45, who has recently separated from Mr. Hanson.

"We'd heard about the girl on the radio," said Ronald Nordhaus, 37, "but it was still a surprise to see her come walking across the corral like that. We had no idea what was going on."

"I'm sure she'll be more careful next time," said his wife, Celeste Nordhaus, 38. "She seemed okay. Hungry and thirsty, though—she ate some scrambled eggs, drank a glass of milk, and she was fast asleep before she said a thing."

The couple did not comment on whether the girl had described her ordeal, and authorities did not say when any answers about what happened might be made public.

"We need some privacy," the girl's mother said. "It's been a hard week and we appreciate everyone's help but we still don't understand what happened and we need to take Helen into consideration before worrying about anyone else's curiosity."

Many hikers and climbers go missing in Mount Rainier National Park. Over the years, there have been almost four hundred fatalities. "Storms roll over the Pacific and shroud Rainier quickly," said Sandy Davidson, a police spokesperson. "The main thing, here, is that the story of Helen Hanson, while a cautionary tale, had a happy ending due to the concerted efforts of law enforcement and volunteers, as well as relatively clear weather."

At Eckstein Middle School, Principal Rebecca Benson said Helen's classmates were eager for her return.

Facsimile

TO B	FROM Helen
COMPANY	COMPANY
FAX (503) 517-7659	FAX (650) 234-2920
SUBJECT	DATE 10.23.2018 2:13 PM

At Sad Clown Lake is where it happened, near the lake
with the white bones showing through the clear water.
The lake was there and the blue tarp stretched above me.
I was in my sleeping bag, on the soft pine branches, the
bed we made. The sun was low, shining through the trees,
and I saw your face in the shadows of that straw hat,
and then you were gone and I was alone in the darkness.
Did I sleep?

Okay, I'm really going to try. I think I can. What do
I know? What do I remember? I do know that we changed
the names on the map. All at once the names come back:
Troublemaker Peak, Monkeyhead River, Big Starling Cairn.
I remember how we found our way, how you blindfolded me
and I led us to Sad Clown Lake.

That time, that night I started telling about, happened
there, in the lean-to, under the blue tarp, next to the
lake where you left me.

I remember at one point that night, getting out of my sleeping bag, out from under the lean-to, and standing in the darkness on the edge of the lake. I shouted and I called for you and the campfire was burned out and you weren't there and no one came. I heard an owl, and I felt like someone was watching me. The full moon was round above, pale yellow, and also on the surface of the lake, and the wind in the trees.

Did I go into the lake? Did I swim? Did I go under? When I woke up, when I found myself (a ridiculous way to describe it, but it feels right to say it that way) it seemed like morning, but after I was found they told me that days, almost a week had gone by. Where were you?

When I awakened I heard the birds in the trees. I rolled over and looked past the edge of the blue tarp, at the gray sky. It was raining. Rain pattered on the surface of the tarp, but not on the lake because there was no lake, no Sad Clown Lake. It had slipped away or I had slipped away, the whole shelter with me, or the lake was never there at all.

You say we were trying to go to a place no one had ever

been. I thought we were searching for Derek, even if you don't remember it that way.

Anyway, the lake was gone when I woke up. I was thirsty, I was starved. We'd left the bottles of water, the dried fish and rice cakes for any passersthrough. I ate the rice cakes and the fish, the granola bars, I drank the water. Perhaps I hadn't had anything to eat or drink for days?

I had lost my clothes, or at least they were gone. I still had my underwear. Again, shouting and calling, no one, not you, no answers. I saw my boots, swinging beneath a tree branch, hanging from their laces. That must be right, because I remember exactly how my bare feet felt in those boots, tightening the laces.

It was cold. Probably it was morning.

I walked in my sleeping bag, which was awkward. I unzipped the bottom zipper and stuck my legs through and kept the top zipped tight around my head. The blue tarp I cut and pulled loose and held somehow like a cape, against the rain. I remember the slippery sound of that sleeping bag and tarp, dragging behind me—I must have looked like a little dragon, or a caterpillar, dragging my tail.

I was eleven. Do you really not know anything about this?

How long, how far did I walk? I know I came to a little stream and followed it down—perhaps you taught me that-believing it would lead somewhere, following the path of the water.

Where the forest ended, there was a wooden fence, and standing there in the trees I looked out onto a pasture and saw this wet, shaggy animal that I didn't recognize, that was somewhat similar to a horse. In that moment I knew I was in a dream or another kind of world, but then the animal turned its neck to look at me and I realized that it was a llama.

Down the slope behind the llama were a small cluster of sheep. They spun and wheeled like a flock of birds when I climbed over the fence—I guess that's why it's called a flock of sheep.

I began to walk down that slope, between those animals, and then I could see the small house with light in its windows and smoke twisting from the chimney.

That's where those people lived who found me, or I found

them. They called, they finally reached Mom, and the way she told me, in her version she just drove out and picked me up.

But was it that fast? Was I not there longer? Were there police? The newspaper article you sent doesn't really answer these questions at all. Do you have other things from back then that you could show me?

I'm not certain if I went straight to the hospital, or if that was later, when they checked me out to be certain that I was all right.

End

Half an hour after they'd pulled away from Benjamin's blue house, Melissa drove her truck through the town of Boring. Benjamin stared out through the window: a feed store, a junkyard; GUIDE DOGS FOR THE BLIND signs flashed by.

"Maybe this isn't the best idea," he said. "I'm not really prepared."

"We're just going for a walk in the woods, Ben. I thought you were retired—now you have somewhere else to be?"

Melissa wore the same necklace, the gray stone at her throat, a pair of jeans, a collared shirt, yellow, with a hole in one elbow. Barefoot. Her hands quick on the steering wheel, she rolled up her window and accelerated, the buffeting air suddenly gone. The window crank on Benjamin's side had been replaced by locking pliers, teeth clamped on the spindle.

"How is it, retirement?" she said. "Lonely?"

"I don't know."

"You miss working?"

"Not exactly," he said. "There were parts I liked—just turning a corner and seeing a person down an aisle, wondering how to fix a leaking faucet, snake a drain, something like that, and being able to help them, to have answers."

"Answers were easier in the world of hardware?" Melissa said, laughing. "Look in that bag—I got something for you. No, that's my backpack. Other one."

In the bag were two pairs of hiking boots; both appeared to be new, with heavy rubber soles, leather and nylon uppers. One blue, one green.

"Try them on," she said. "They're different sizes."

The dog began barking, the sound echoing in the camper topper behind them.

"He'll stop barking and fall asleep," she said, "once we're out on the highway."

Benjamin leaned forward, tore the Velcro of his sandal loose from one ankle, then the other. The boots' laces were tied together, and he had to use his teeth to loosen them. Pain shot through his face; he sat up, closed his eyes.

"Easy," she said.

Alongside his leg, the seat's faded fabric was lined with dark stains that he suspected were his blood, from the last time he rode in the truck. He forced his foot into one boot, stretched his leg out straight, pressing against the floorboard. Out the window, trees blurred together. A broken-down farm slid past. He stretched out his hand and ran his fingers along a crescent of indentations in the dashboard, a matching set underneath, where he couldn't see. Teeth marks. The small mouth of a child.

"You have any children?" he said.

"Excuse me?"

"I was just wondering." He tapped the dashboard, set his hand back in his lap.

"Children?" Melissa said. "Not that I know of. I guess I could—could be some out there, somewhere."

"What?"

"That was a joke." She straightened her fingers against the steering wheel, accelerated onto the highway. "And you, just the one daughter? No, that's not right—you also had a son."

"Derek," he said. "Yes. He died when he was a boy."

The wind ruffling between the cab and the camper, the tires humming on the highway. The dog was silent now, as Melissa had promised.

"So how are they?" she said.

"Well, only Helen is left," he said. "She's doing well, I think—I've seen more of her, lately; there was a long time when I didn't know if I'd ever see her again."

"I meant the boots."

"Oh," he said. "The green ones are better, I think."

. . .

THEY PASSED THROUGH Zigzag, then Rhododendron, and began to climb. Mount Hood loomed overhead, then folded itself away again in the clouds.

Leaning back, Melissa straightened her legs and arms as if urging the truck, its engine straining, up the incline; then she turned off the highway, rattling along a gravel path that turned into a dirt road. Swooping through the deep shadows under the trees, they soon arrived at a picnic area, the parking lot almost full. People stood in clusters near tables, around fire pits; a banner, stretched between two trees, read THATCHER FAMILY REUNION.

Melissa opened her door and hopped out of the truck. She swung her pack over one shoulder, picking up a red coil of rope that had been hidden beneath it.

"Well?" she said.

He opened his door and climbed down, slid his walking stick from behind the seat.

"Colder up here," he said.

Melissa was wearing a jean jacket, now, with a shearling collar. She pulled a down vest from her pack, held it out to him.

"Have gloves for you, if you want them," she said. "But once we get walking, we'll warm up. Now, your wrist-watch."

"What?"

"Give it to me."

She held out her hand, then put the watch in her pocket. Next, she took out a sheathed knife he hadn't noticed before, then a mace canister, attaching it to a holster on her belt. When she opened the camper's door, a clatter immediately rose up within, and Johnson's black and gray snout appeared, sticking through the gap. He growled at Benjamin, then went quiet as Melissa lay her hand atop his head. She tied the red rope around the dog's neck.

"Just stand here next to me," Melissa said to Benjamin. "Stay still."

The black dog bounded, whining, lunging at his feet, almost knocking him over.

"Johnson!" Melissa said, and the dog looked up, then sat down. Now she wrapped her arms around Benjamin's middle and hugged him close. "Look, boy—this is my

friend. He's mine. He is the same as me. We're the same."
She spoke slowly. "Ben didn't mean to startle you, the other
day. You'll treat him like you treat me."

As they walked along the edge of the picnic area, small
dogs began yapping; Johnson stood on his hind legs, then
let out one low bark, and they went silent.

"Here, Ben. This way."

Soon they could no longer see the people around the
picnic tables, the parking lot far behind. The dog strained
at the end of the rope, veered from one side of the trail
to the other, all the while glancing sidelong at Benjamin.
Squirrels leapt from branch to branch; birds shot through
the spaces between trees, out into the sky.

"Do you ever get that feeling," Melissa said, "when
you're looking up at a bird, like a hawk sliding up in
the air currents, that your feet aren't even touching the
ground? It also hits you, here." She tapped at the center
of Benjamin's chest.

"I don't know," he said. "I guess so."

"You hear these birds, warning each other, saying we're
coming?" she said. "It's good to be out here. Already, don't
you think? Oh, thimbleberries." She knelt down next to the
path, picking at the bushes, then held out her palm, full of
pink berries.

He took one, put it in his mouth, crushed its sourness

between his teeth. Melissa was already striding ahead of him; he hurried to catch up.

"One time," she said. "This was years ago, when I was living with Janice, my big sister, far away in a forest. We saw an owl drop straight out of the sky—it was dusk—and take a rabbit. It was amazing, so quick and silent, like it just appeared in the air. And back then we were starving, hadn't had meat for days, so we ran at it, dragging these sticks, this tree branch, and the owl was huge with its wings stretched out, atop the rabbit. Johnson was barking—he was there, then, just a puppy, he was Janice's dog—and that owl was so stubborn, kept coming back, but finally we drove it off, and took the rabbit—"

A clattering, in the bushes to the right; the dog chased something, then returned, running parallel to them. Melissa offered a hand as Benjamin climbed up a root, around a tree. Her hand was rough, callused; it felt tender and awkward, their arms swinging together for a moment before she let go.

"We skinned and roasted that rabbit over the fire," she said. "It was delicious. We were so pleased with ourselves, bellies full, and then I stood up from my fire and it was like *wham*"—she slapped the top of her head—"and I thought I'd been struck by lightning, or a tree branch, because it was so sharp, and then those feathers, the wings clapping all around my head, and it wouldn't let go! So I reached up and got hold of it, and it was biting—is biting the right word?—my fingers, but finally I broke its wing, I think, and then I threw it into the fire, and it came right out, half flying, smoldering, crashing out into the trees.

"We never found the owl," Melissa said, after a pause, "which was strange, but I was bleeding so much, and I was probably in shock."

Laughing, she swung her pack around, unzipped it. When she held out a water bottle, he unscrewed the top, took a drink. Water spilled down his chin, wet the collar of his shirt.

"Look." She kneeled in front of him, holding her hair flat, parting it along the crown of her head to show a thick white scar. "That's where the owl hit me. Janice put that same poultice on this wound—she's the one who taught me about it—and it healed right up."

"Where's she now?" he said. "Your sister?"

"She's dead." Melissa screwed the top back on the water bottle, and stuffed it into her pack. "Three years ago, last summer. She died in a fire."

Benjamin looked down at his boots, their bright red laces; when he looked up, Melissa was already walking away, the black soles of her feet flashing.

. . .

THEY CAME TO a clearing. One tall, bare tree leaned against lush pines, like the skeleton of a giant fish standing on its tail. Melissa turned to face him, then bent down and untied the rope from the dog's neck—it leapt forward, snarling, but Melissa stepped close, put her arms around Benjamin. The dog bounded away, into the underbrush.

"How you feeling?" she said, loosening her arms, stepping away.

"Okay," he said. "A little winded."

"Here." She took hold of his walking stick and leaned it against a tree.

"I need that," he said.

"We can get it on the way back."

"You have a map?"

"Here, this is edible. Miner's lettuce." She held out a handful.

"I know that," he said, but didn't take the leaves.

Somewhere they couldn't see, the dog barked once; there was a crashing in the underbrush, followed by a voice.

"Come out!" Melissa called, looking past Benjamin. "I know you're there. I've known it the whole time."

Silence. Benjamin heard water running, somewhere, but he couldn't see its source. And then the bushes shook, thirty feet away, the leaves' disturbance moving gradually toward the trail. Slowly, a figure emerged, followed by the dog, its tail wagging.

"Cisco," Melissa said. "We talked about this."

It was the same boy, the one who had had the white bicycle, who had worn the yellow gloves. He wasn't wearing gloves now, his palms flashing as he held them up, explaining.

"I didn't know you were going to drive so far." The boy wore camouflage pants, a dirty blue jacket. "How was I supposed to know?"

"We talked about this last night."

"Melissa—"

"We've also talked about you following me," she said, "and being in my truck. Unless you're invited, it's not okay."

"I know. I know we did talk about that."

"Now, you have two choices," she said. "You can walk back and wait at the truck, or you can hitchhike home."

"Can I at least take Johnson?"

"Yes, but he's tired." Melissa threw the coil of red rope at the boy's feet. "Now, go."

No one spoke for a moment, and then the boy picked up the rope, called the dog. The two of them disappeared back down the trail.

"He's a little insecure," Melissa said. "Jealous. Come on."

She reached out, plucked at Benjamin's shirt, turned away. They walked on, under the trees, the trail becoming less distinct beneath their feet.

"Somehow I'm less tired than I was before," he said.

"That's good. That's a good sign."

"We're not lost?"

"No, we're not lost," she said.

"How far are we going? Are we circling around?"

"A little," she said. "Here."

The path began to descend; she reached out and took his arm, from time to time, to steady him. Light filtered through the trees, shifting shadows around them. He glanced upward, thinking of owls.

"If it was me," Melissa said, "if I lost someone I cared about and there was any way that I could reach her, I'd find them, whatever it took."

"What?"

"I keep thinking about it," she said. "About your daughter."

"I did try to find her," he said. "I was leading these people all through the forest where she and I had been. Exactly where we'd been." Benjamin paused, caught his breath. "And everyone was questioning me, and I couldn't lead them to anything like what I said I could."

. . .

FIRST THEY SAW the colors—blue, red, silver—of vehicles, glinting through the trees, and then heard the laughter and voices, becoming more distinct.

The people were spread out now, flames leaping in the rings of stones. On one edge, the boy, Cisco, sat alone at a picnic table, a paper plate and a can of Coke in front of him, the dog asleep at his feet. The boy stood up when he saw them approaching; even from a distance, Benjamin could see the redness of his face, angry, his freckles brought into relief. Melissa was stepping quickly to him, but he was looking past her, at Benjamin, as he began to shout.

"You don't even know!" he said. "You think she even likes you? You're getting so worked!"

Now the people at the family reunion were looking over.

"Did you even notice that she stole your computer?" Cisco said. "She even told me to go to your house today, since you'd be gone, and see what else we could take. Those tools, in your basement—I was going to score some of those—"

"Cisco," Melissa said.

"And the other night," the boy said, "the other night we even took your car, while you were sleeping, drove it all over the city."

"We brought it back," Melissa said, then turned away from Benjamin—her voice low, earnest—and started saying something to Cisco; in a moment, the boy stood, clearly pouting as he dragged his feet to the back of the camper. He opened the door, let the dog jump in, then disappeared inside as well. He slammed the door shut.

Melissa gestured to Benjamin, urging him to hurry.

"Onlookers," she said, as he climbed up into the passenger seat.

Benjamin looked out at the people clustered around the picnic tables, and they looked back. The truck's engine rattled and coughed, and then they were moving, the ground sliding away even before he got his door closed.

Out under the trees, onto the highway, downhill and pointed toward home, the truck leaning hard around the corners.

"You took my computer?" he said.

"I did. On the day we met." Melissa's voice didn't change; she didn't turn to look at him, just gazed through the windshield like they were talking about nothing. "What, you want it back?"

"You didn't ask," he said.

"What would you have said? You were asleep, incapacitated. And I need it more than you do. I can use it. I mean, you hadn't even opened the box."

"And my car?" he said.

"We had some errands to run," she said. "And I was

teaching Cisco to drive; I can't very well do that in this truck."

"You were what?"

"He's fifteen," she said. "Stop shouting. Why are you so angry?"

"You lied to me."

"I did things you didn't know about," she said. "That's different than lying to you."

They drove through Rhododendron, Zigzag, the highway leveling out.

"You didn't tell me things you should've told me," Benjamin said. "That's pretty much the same thing as lying."

Leaning forward, he untied, then loosened his boots. He jerked them from his feet, struggling to pull his sandals out from beneath the seat. When he glanced up, over at Melissa, she wasn't looking at him. She stared straight ahead, her jaw tense.

Silence. They slowed, eased through Sandy, the stores built up along the highway. McDonald's, Fred Meyer, Safeway, Schoolhouse Pharmacy.

"Those things, whatever, those aren't really things that matter." Melissa pointed ahead, through the windshield, as if gesturing to the future.

He turned away, watching as the rain began to fall out of the gray sky.

"My watch," he said.

"What?"

"You still have my watch."

Melissa reached into her pocket and threw it in his lap.

"Were you going to give that back?" he said.

"You honestly think I care about your watch?"

·   ·   ·

THEY DIDN'T SPEAK again until they'd reached the outskirts of the city, almost to Benjamin's house.

"Sad Clown Lake," Melissa said, the words slow. "At Sad Clown Lake is where it happened. Near the lake with the white bones showing through." She glanced at Benjamin. "But what happened at Sad Clown Lake? Helen wanted to find her brother. The lake disappeared, and she went missing?"

"That wasn't for you," Benjamin said. "What she sent me. We don't know what happened, really. I don't."

"Sad Clown Lake—"

"Stop. You don't even know what you're talking about."

He reached to open the window, to get fresh air; his hand knocked the pliers free from the spindle and they landed sharply on his stockinged foot.

Benjamin: So much of what you say or write is about what I don't know, when I wasn't there, where I wasn't. The parts where I was there, I don't know if you remember it all? For instance, you haven't really talked about the passersthrough, and what about the notebook?

+

We left the lean-to out in the forest, we stopped taking it apart, to see what would happen, and we left the notebook in the lean-to. That was your idea, to leave it there, to see if anyone would write in it. The first time, there were only the dirty words, and then the beer cans and trash all around the lean-to. But later when we went deeper, when I followed you in your blindfold, the lean-to wasn't so easy for people to find. And then Sad Clown Lake was sometimes there, sometimes not, and there were messages from hikers and Boy Scouts, and then, later, those pencil drawings that were so precise, of bones and trees and trees made out of bones? With those shaky lines around everything that looked like movement or wind or sound?

+

That's where you started talking about the pass-ersthrough as a kind of person different from us, who might need something or draw those drawings, who might be trying to reach us. And you were the one who wanted to leave the lean-to out there, who thought we could always find it. The first few times we set it up and I took it all down again.

+

Benjamin: Five days have gone by since I've heard from you and that makes me worry.

+

Maybe I've been too pushy, trying to find out every-thing that happened, what went wrong, and it's been so much, so fast, after so little for so long. What's important—what's important is I want you to trust me again, to know that I'm sorry for all this time we've been apart, to say that whatever happened wasn't something I did. Not something I planned or understood.

+

Also, there are times before what happened that are important, that I don't want to forget. I remember how it was, how it felt to be reading a book with the warmth of you on one side and Derek on the other, sitting together on our orange couch with the chill coming through the glass of the window behind us. That was such a drafty house. The two of you leaned against me before you could even read, and I read you so many things. I remember *Frog and Toad,* especially the one where Toad is sad because he never gets mail, so Frog runs home and writes a letter to Toad, then gives it to a snail to deliver and runs back to Toad's house to wait for the letter to arrive. I can't even remember what that letter said.

+

And then I would finish reading the book and you would fall asleep, if you hadn't already. Derek would be asleep. I'd pick him up and carry him back to his room, to his bed.

+

You used to talk in your sleep. Sometimes back when we lived in the same house, when you were a girl, I heard your voice and so I climbed the stairs, went down the hallway and stood outside the door of your bedroom. I heard you say your brother's name. Derek, Derek. This was after he died, and before I had to move away. I wonder if you still talk in your sleep.

+

The other night I had a dream that a swarm of bees attacked a herd of cattle, and the cows ran in every direction across the bright fields.

+

Your brother Derek was quiet and you were not quiet. You wouldn't sleep and you'd cry and cry, couldn't be consoled. The more we tried to calm you down, the more you cried–I remember wrapping you in the little blanket, swaddling you, and there was no wrap you couldn't fight your way out of. Houdini, we called you. You cried, and the only thing that worked was one time I was so exhausted, exasperated that I started copying you, pretending to cry, and immediately you stopped, and your expression got so worried, your little face, your brow all furrowed, and you reached out your tiny arms to comfort me.

+

Sometimes when I think of your brother I suspect I'm imagining or inventing as much as I'm remembering.

We knew him for only seven years, and even then he was shy, so quiet, such a quiet baby, a sound sleeper. We were always checking to be certain that he was alive, still breathing, which seems terrible, ironic, even if no amount of checking would have stopped what happened, whatever it was, no one could ever say.

+

Do you know when you might come visit again?

+

Facsimile

TO B	FROM Helen
COMPANY	COMPANY
FAX (503) 517-7659	FAX (650) 234-2920
SUBJECT	DATE 10.29.2018 9:17 PM

I didn't mean to make you worry. I'm not overwhelmed by our conversation, not yet. I meant to write before now, but work has been crazy. I had to fly to San Diego, then New Jersey. I'm typing this on a plane, actually, returning from the East Coast. I'm probably somewhere over Utah or Nevada. I'm listening to your voice on my earphones. I'll fax this to you when I'm back on the ground, home again.

Sometimes if I'm driving or washing dishes I'll just play back your voice, to hear you talking. Your voice has changed a little, since I was a girl, since you've gotten older, or maybe I just remember it wrong. I keep the transcriptions of all you've said in a folder with the birthday cards.

Hiding in the leaves I don't remember, but I do remember one time when you and Mom were having a party and all the guests' coats were piled on your bed and me and Derek crawled under them and waited. He might have fallen asleep. I remember the weight of the coats, and the smell of wool, of perfume. The sounds of voices and music and laughter. Sometimes a person would come in and take their coat, and the weight would be lighter.

Some of my happiest memories are when I'd be in my bed in my bedroom at night, when I was a girl, and I could hear you and Mom laughing in the kitchen. The low sound of your voices, and then laughing together. It was a happy sound.

Wasn't Frog's letter to Toad simply about how much he appreciated having Toad for a best friend?

You used to tell us about how when you were a kid you'd run through the forest, you'd escape your parents, how you'd spend whole days in the trees, not touching the ground. You had all kinds of stories, like the one about how you found a snake frozen so stiff you could hold it out like a stick, a wand, but then you took it inside by the fire and it warmed up and thawed and sang a song. Do you remember that song? Part of it was about how much it tickled your lips to have a forked tongue that was constantly going in and out, so when you sang it your tongue would be going in and out all the time. Derek and I laughed and laughed.

End

Another day came and went, then another, and another. It was only midafternoon, getting dark already. November. The leaves of the elms, mostly gone, revealed birds' nests in the branches high above. Jack-o'-lanterns rotted on porches, a deflated witch hung from a lamppost, a sagging yarn spiderweb across a doorway.

Benjamin walked between black puddles shot through with rainbows of gasoline. He hadn't seen Melissa since the day of the hike, and he didn't know if he would, if he wanted to. There was no sign of her—even her truck was missing, not out in front of the abandoned house, where he found himself, now, standing in the rutted mud.

A sign read NO TRESPASSING. And the house numbers looked somehow wrong. He stepped closer, saw that they'd been pried loose, flipped and reversed, roughly reattached:

He knocked, waited, then tried the doorknob. Locked.

Back at the hardware store, Winks, they'd had cross sections of doors with all kinds of locks and knobs, all down one side, for demonstration purposes. Sometimes, when things were slow, he and his workmates would practice picking the locks, twisting wires in, sliding credit cards into the gap. But he had no wire here, nothing for the dead bolt.

He hurried out from under the porch's overhang, back into the rain; blackberry vines tangled around his feet as he made his way toward the side door, which he found unlocked.

Closing the door behind him, he skirted the hole in the floor, the darkness below.

"Hello?" He did not raise his voice, but it echoed through the rooms.

The bedroom where he had been before, with Melissa, was still flooded with green light, the window thick with blackberry vines, snarled and pressing against the glass. There was no orange electrical cord snaking in, no telephone or computers, no jugs of water. Only the plastic folding chair, the painted white dresser propped up with the phone book.

He pulled out the dresser's top drawer, and there was

a clatter of plastic and metal, settling. At least twenty cell phones lay jumbled together amid tangles of cords and plugs.

The second drawer was full of folded clothes—T-shirts, yellow and pink sweaters. He pulled out a sweater, held it up: it was so small, clearly for a child. Folding it, he placed it back as it had been, then checked the bottom drawer. One tiny blue sneaker, two small pairs of jeans.

He pushed the drawers closed, leaning in with his knees, and then stood still for a moment, listening, the silence of the house all around him. The rain suddenly picked up, heavy on the rooftop, a darker sound in the house. He shivered, then headed out the other door, into the hallway.

In the second bedroom, the metal rectangle of a bed frame rested on the floor. No mattress, no box spring. A wooden chair, its back charred, scorch marks on the wall. He turned away without going inside.

The stairs stretched down, at the end of the hallway. Slowly, his eyes adjusting, he checked each stair with his foot before he stepped. The sound of his wet socks, squishing in his sandals. At the bottom, on the concrete floor, plastic tape stretched and tangled on itself: POLICE LINE DO NOT CROSS.

To the right, the dark, hulking square shape of a furnace. To the left, the slanting light from the hole in the kitchen floor overhead.

Benjamin stepped carefully across the floor, unable to see his feet, until he was standing in the light. He tilted his face upward to look through the hole, at the faded ceiling of the kitchen, the pale circle of the light fixture and the darker shadows of the lightbulbs inside it.

The sound of the door, then, scraping open above him. Benjamin stood still; above, through the jagged hole, a silhouette, a hooded figure.

"Someone in here?"

The voice, a boy's voice, echoed in the house. It was a familiar voice, though it took Benjamin a moment to realize that it was Cisco, standing in the kitchen, now kneeling down, squinting into the basement.

"You fell down there?"

"No," Benjamin said. "I came down the stairs."

"What're you doing?"

"Nothing."

"You're not doing nothing."

"I thought . . ." Benjamin said. "I thought maybe Melissa would be here. I was looking for her."

"You thought you'd find Melissa?" The boy stood again, his face hidden in the shadows of his hood. "You don't know anything, boss! She said no one could be here anymore, that something was going to happen."

"But you're here," Benjamin said.

"If you knew anything," Cisco said, "if you knew any-thing about Melissa, you'd see that if Melissa wants you to find her, she'll find you. She'll find you! You're not going to just find her like that."

Cisco clapped his hands to his sides, then stepped side-ways, out of view. His footsteps made the ceiling creak; they walked away, and then there was silence.

Back up the stairs, down the hallway, Benjamin started into the bedroom, the light dim; Cisco stood there, his wet sweatshirt half over his head, cursing as he struggled to pull it off, finally slapping it onto the floor.

"I just came back for my last things," he said, glancing at Benjamin. "I never liked it here—it's creepy, after what happened. I never would've come in here, after that."

"After what?"

"What do you even know about anything? Nothing!" Cisco crawled across the floor, reached under the dresser and jerked out a backpack; unzipping it, he pulled out another sweatshirt, a yellow rain slicker.

"This house," he said. "It's a murder house. They call it 'Hell House' because of the numbers. It was two kids, their mother—she did it, she did it to them."

"In this house?"

"Of course in this freaking house—that's what I'm saying." Cisco rubbed his wet hair, found an orange stocking cap, pulled it on. "They were just kids, man, I maybe even saw them around on the street, you know? And now they're gone."

Cisco looked around the room as if to be certain not to forget anything. The green blackberry vines and leaves trembled and scratched against the window, struck by the rain, which was slanting down hard.

"So Melissa said something's going to happen here?" Benjamin said.

"I don't know what. She knows, I guess."

"Where is she?"

"Somewhere," Cisco said. "But you're not going to find her because she doesn't need to find you. She doesn't want to be found by you, you know? She told me, boss—she told me we're going camping, me and her. So when she finds someone, that person's going to be me, not you."

With that, Cisco turned and went back out the door, the kitchen. The door slapped, the sound of rain suddenly rising up.

. . .

AS HE APPROACHED his house, sloshing through the puddles, Benjamin saw a flash of red in the rhododendrons below the bedroom window—Javier, shuffling from the bushes, running to his own house. Benjamin turned down the driveway, went through the gate.

Had he left the door to the kitchen unlocked? He stepped inside, hung up his raincoat on its hook, loosened his sandals' straps. He had to sit on the floor to pull off his socks, and as he stood to wring them out in the sink he noticed that the light over the stairs, down to the basement, was on. Turning it off, he listened to the silence, decided not to descend.

As he stepped into the living room, however, he heard a gentle splashing, the sound of water.

"Hello?"

No answer. He moved toward the bedroom, where light slanted from the window to a tangle of clothes, strewn inside out on the floor. A familiar canvas bag. Again, the splash of water, the sound of breathing behind the closed bathroom door.

"Melissa?" he said, leaning there. "Is that you?"

"Yes."

"You're in the bathtub?"

"Obviously," she said.

He sat down on his bed. He pulled out the drawer of his dresser, leaned forward and took a dry pair of socks from the drawer.

"I was looking for you," he said.

"Well, here I am."

Outside, the sound of a car passing. Silence again.

"So I come home," he said, "and you're taking a bath in my house."

"Evidently." Her voice echoed off the tiles, a hint of her husky laugh behind the words.

Benjamin pulled on one sock, stretched to reach the other, which had fallen under the bed.

"Today," he said. "That house—the one where you were before, where I found you that time—"

"On Sixty-Sixth?"

"You never told me what happened there."

"The murders, you mean? Why would I tell you about that?"

"When—" he said. "How long ago did that happen?"

"Not so long. A month?" There were larger splashes, behind the door; Melissa was standing, getting out of the bath. "I was thinking," she said, "wondering if we might take a little drive. Just up into Washington."

"I'm not sure I want to go anywhere with you," he said.

"You're still sulking?"

"You stole from me," he said, "and now, you break into my house."

"I have a key," she said. "That's not exactly 'breaking in.'"

Benjamin stood, stepped to the doorway, looked across

at the two machines on the table, the stack of paper, Helen's faxes on the windowsill. Behind him, the bathroom door opened, and Melissa stepped out, through a cloud of steam. She wore a gray suit jacket, a matching skirt. When she unwrapped the towel from her head, her hair was shorter, darker, all one color.

"You look different," he said.

"You like it?"

"I don't know."

"Well, *you* look much better." She touched his shoulder, gently moved around him. "You took off the bandage."

"Yes."

"It's all right if we take your Subaru?" She was in the bathroom again, leaning close to the mirror, putting on lipstick. "I got everything ready to go."

Melissa twirled the car key around her finger as Benjamin opened the door on the passenger side.

"No," she said, "get in the back with Johnson. He's going to whine and carry on if he's back there alone."

The dog, hearing his name, leapt up and began barking, claws scrabbling at the window.

"How about he rides in front?" Benjamin said.

"Fine. Let's just get going."

They accelerated away from the house, through the neighborhood, under the streetlights. The rain eased, and the windshield wipers began to scrape; it took a moment for Melissa to figure out how to turn them off.

"We're headed to visit these two." She pulled a news-paper clipping from her pocket, waved it over her shoulder. "Up in Klickitat. See what they remember about Helen." She set the article on the dashboard and the defrost fan blew it onto the passenger seat; Johnson sniffed it. "What they say in there feels a little off to me—and the time is hard to track, especially when you add in all those faxes of Helen's."

"Why?" he said. "You took that from my house?"

"Where else would I get it?"

"They're probably not even there," he said. "That's twenty-five years ago."

"They are," she said. "I checked."

"Did you talk to them?"

Melissa shook her head.

"So they don't know we're coming."

"Element of surprise."

They kept driving, out of Woodstock, through sparse traffic. Johnson lay his head on the back of the seat, staring at Benjamin, then suddenly clambered over. His tail slapped Benjamin's chest, then his snout was in his face.

"See, he's warming up to you," Melissa said. "Maybe crack the window for him, a little."

The dog stood on Benjamin's lap, one paw on each thigh, his snout out the window. The buffeting sound, the dampness of rain filled the car.

Streetlamps cast light through the windshield; he could see Melissa's smile in the rearview mirror. She wasn't wearing her usual necklace. With her hair cut so short, it was easier to see her face, her neck, the two black X's of the tattoo behind her ear.

"So is your brother going to my house?" he said. "While we're gone?"

"Cisco?" she said. "Not that I know of."

"Could you at least not take the fax machine, or the other one?"

"Stop being so suspicious."

"I just saw him, actually," Benjamin said.

"Cisco?"

"At the house."

"Was he following you?"

"I don't think so," Benjamin said. "I don't know. But it was him that told me about the children, the murders."

"Ah."

"And then he told me you were taking him camping."

Melissa laughed. "I told him I *might* take him camping."

They were driving across the long bridge, the dark waters of the Columbia beneath them. Benjamin glanced back at Oregon, receding, then turned to look out through the windshield, at Washington, as they approached it.

"What are we even going to say to these people?" he said.

"Mostly I want to listen, ask them some questions, see what they remember about Helen. We'll see. I mean, what does this newspaper say? 'One unexplained detail is how

Helen was found a hundred miles from where her father claimed she was last seen.'"

They were in Washington, now, driving east along the Columbia. To the right, the river's black water glinted in the moonlight. The square, dark shapes of barges plowed through the night. Melissa's phone illuminated her face as she checked the map, glancing down, up again.

"I mean, how to explain it?" she said. "Moving lakes and traveling lean-tos, I guess."

"I never told anyone that," Benjamin said.

"What did you tell them?"

"Everything I could," he said. "Which wasn't very much, I guess, really. I woke up in the morning, and Helen wasn't there. The whole lean-to was gone, too, but I didn't tell them that." He rolled down the window more—rain sliced in, the dog raised his head—and rolled it up again. "It was impossible," he said. "Impossible to get anyone to believe me, that I hadn't done some terrible thing."

"But you don't remember everything."

"I do remember everything," he said. "I just couldn't find her. Where she went, I don't know that, but I never knew it."

· · ·

MELISSA FLICKED ON the high beams, the trees along the highway leaning up, silvery, for an instant. The dog shifted, asleep, one hind leg bent up over Benjamin's lap, the rough black pads of his foot upturned.

. . .

ON THROUGH WHITE Salmon, they drove past Bingen, turned on 142 before Lyle, the highway following the dark curves of the Klickitat River, then onto a smaller road; Melissa slowed to swerve around potholes and the headlights bounced to one side—panning across silhouettes of tree trunks, a thick forest—and then away, the shadows rushing back in.

"So how do we start?" Benjamin said. "What will we say?"

Melissa didn't answer. She turned left, then slowed, switching off the headlights. They crept another several hundred yards along a gravel road before easing to a stop.

Ahead, the dark outline of a house, blue flickering television light glowing from one window. There were no surrounding houses, no neighbors.

Melissa squinted at the newspaper, then glanced through the windshield.

"Looks the same," she said. "Doesn't it?"

"A couple more satellite dishes on the roof," he said, "but yes, it's the same house."

"I'll be right back."

She took a flashlight from the glove compartment, opened her door—sliding out quickly—and closed it again quietly, the light on the ceiling winking to life for only an instant. Johnson, suddenly awake, whined, ears slapping as he shook his head.

Benjamin could only see the pale circle of light, sliding along the ground, illuminating the small area around Melissa—her boots stepping over a broken fence, through the remnants of a corral, past what looked like pieces of a snow-mobile.

Alongside the house, the pale circle darted up the wall, slashed back to the silvery grass: Melissa was jumping, he realized, trying to see through the window.

Now the beam zigzagged, her dark figure behind it, ducking low as she ran back to the car.

"Everything's perfect," she said.

The car door was open, her eyes shining; the gap between her teeth was familiar, but her short, dark hair made her look like someone else.

"Come," she said. "You don't really have to say much at all. Play along with me. Let me get them talking."

He climbed out, followed her around puddles, then up

an overgrown path to the front door. As they approached, the sound of voices, of music, grew louder. She reached back to touch his shoulder.

"Play along," she said, her voice a whisper.

When she knocked on the door, all at once there was silence, then footsteps, slowly approaching.

The door opened—light spilled out, around a woman, her face in shadow. Her white hair hung in two braids, resting in front of her shoulders.

"Celeste Nordhaus?" Melissa said.

"Yes?" The woman squinted out at them. She held something—a piece of black plastic, a remote control—in one hand.

"We'd like to talk with you."

"About what?"

"I'm Helen Hanson," Melissa said.

"Who?"

"I'm sure you remember my name." She held up the newspaper article, and the woman leaned closer. "And this is my father, Ben."

Behind them, Johnson began barking, his dark shape shifting around inside the shadowy car. The old woman looked out, past them, shielding her eyes. Melissa turned and pointed at the car, a quick, insistent motion; Johnson went quiet, still.

Now a stooped, gaunt man appeared behind the woman. Old, but younger than Benjamin. Unruly white hair, tangled eyebrows, reading glasses on a cord around his neck.

"Ron, it's the girl," the woman said. "She's come back."

"The girl?"

"Helen Hanson," Melissa said. "Are you going to invite us in?"

"What do you want?"

"To talk."

The woman, Celeste, stepped aside; Benjamin followed Melissa up the two concrete steps, through a mudroom. A white cat leapt off a couch in the next room, slithered through a doorway. A nature program played on the large, muted television—a cougar with her two spotted cubs played outside a snowy den, the words DEPENDENT ON THEIR MOTHER FOR A YEAR scrolling beneath them.

"Well," Celeste said.

She and Ron and Melissa and Benjamin all stood between the back of the couch and the doorway to the dim kitchen. The room was hot, a fire in a woodstove, the smell of smoke. Both Ron and Celeste wore green down vests, despite the heat.

"It's late, to visit," Ron said. "Did you peek in the window, just now?"

"That was me," Melissa said.

"Celeste said I was being ridiculous," he said, "but I thought I saw someone."

"I just wanted to check that you were here," Melissa said. "That you didn't have guests or something."

Benjamin accidentally brushed against Celeste, who quickly pulled away; the space was so tight, their four bodies together.

"This is unexpected," Ron said. "That was so long ago."

"I just wanted to talk about what happened," Melissa said. "Ask a few questions, for my own sake."

"That's the story." Celeste gestured at the scrap of newspaper, still in Melissa's hand. "That's all that happened, and now, our memories aren't so sharp—"

"That's why we came to talk to you," Melissa said. "Because what it says in the newspaper isn't exactly what happened, is it? It feels like there's more; I feel like there's more. So maybe our memories can help each other?"

"I don't know," Ron said.

"We were hoping that you could help us, talk it through."

Melissa held out the newspaper article again, and Ron took it. He put on his reading glasses, and Celeste leaned close to read it, as well.

In the silence, Benjamin looked down at Ron's red wool socks; one big toe, a yellow toenail poking through. He looked up at a leaning bookcase of snow globes, the faded yellow spines of *National Geographic*s, at the black windows that reflected pieces of the room, the bright colors of the cougars eating a fresh kill, then back to his own hands, clutched in front of him.

"A lot of it doesn't make sense to me," Melissa said. "The timing, for one thing. And you don't know how hard it was, on some people, what you did and didn't do, what you didn't say. My father, here—he lost all custody, all visitation rights, because of what happened."

The cat's white face flashed for a moment in the door to the hallway, disappeared again.

"But you're together now," Ron said.

"After we were apart for a long time. After he was blamed—"

"This is our house." Celeste, now standing in the kitchen, took a yellow phone off the wall. "Maybe you should just leave."

"We'll be gone soon enough," Melissa said. "We'll talk this one time, and then we'll go away. After all, you don't want other people to get involved again, after so long, to have to tell what you did and didn't do."

Celeste hung up the phone, its long, yellow cord twisting back on itself.

Stepping around the couch, Benjamin sat down in an

easy chair; what he thought was a lamp, next to him, turned out to be some kind of cat furniture, covered in carpeting.

Suddenly Celeste stuck out her hand, startling him, but she was only switching off the television. With that, the atmosphere in the room began to quiet and settle. She sat on the couch, her husband next to her.

"So," Melissa said. She was sitting in a rocking chair, next to the stove, crossing her legs, smoothing her skirt. "Can we start at the beginning? I just came wandering out of the woods, across the corral?"

"You did come across the corral," Ron said, "just like in the newspaper. Isn't that how it tells it? I really think that's likely all the story you need."

"But it's so short," Melissa said. "The article. I bet we might remember some details, if we think through it."

The silence gathered. Benjamin felt it in the air, a tension against his skin and crackle in his ears. Melissa sat with her hands on her knees, rocking slightly; she faced the couple on the couch with an expectant expression, as if she would wait them out. They sat there looking uncomfortable in their puffy green vests.

"You came right across the corral," Ron said, "just exactly like that."

"Well, not exactly," Celeste said.

"Not exactly what?" said Melissa.

"That's what happened, it just doesn't really say how."

"Did you know who I was?"

"No."

"You didn't know I was missing? You hadn't read anything about Helen Hanson?"

The room had grown hotter. Benjamin's head felt heavy; when Melissa said Helen's name, he realized that he'd forgotten it was Melissa—not that he thought it was Helen; she seemed more like a third person, someone who existed only in this place and time. Leaning forward, he unzipped his jacket, shucked it off behind him.

"We didn't know," Celeste said. "We didn't know who you were until later, after we called the police. That part of the newspaper is wrong."

"So why did you say you knew who I was?"

"Let them tell it," Benjamin said. "Back to the beginning. Don't interrupt." He smiled at the couple on the couch. "So, she came out of the trees, across the corral."

"Right," Ron said. "The animals were running, they were spooked by her. By you."

"How do you remember it?" Celeste said, pointing at Melissa. "Is that what you remember?"

"I'll know if you're telling it right," Melissa said. "I'll tell you if it feels wrong."

Outside, a distant dog barked. It didn't sound like

Johnson. The window reflected the room back into the room, the four of them, sitting there.

"When she," Ron said, "when you came out of the trees, you weren't quite walking—"

"What it was was you were crawling," Celeste said, "with your legs and arms straight, not bent, though, and sometimes you'd flip over with your neck bent back, skittering, not moving in a straight line at all. We still talk about it sometimes, how weird it was, like not a human being way to move. And you weren't hardly wearing any clothes at all but that blue tarp with a hole cut in it, like a poncho, and only one shoe, I think."

"It wasn't easy to catch you," Ron said, "even though you were aimed at the house, coming to us. I had to wrestle you around and you were stronger than how I expected a girl should be. You remember that?"

"Go on," Melissa said.

Celeste bent forward, pulled a basket of yarn with two bright metal needles sticking out around closer to her feet, then sat back on the couch again.

"We were afraid," she said. "Your eyes, it was like they were the opposite of crossed, like each one was pointed way out to the side of your head and you were acting like what you were seeing was not what we were seeing. You were just kind of growling, but you were hungry."

"You ate everything," Ron said. "Eggs, flour—nothing even had to be cooked."

"It was like you could see everything in your side vision—"

"Peripheral vision."

"Yes, you could see to the side and even behind you, just not straight ahead."

"And that's when you called the police?" Melissa said.

"Well, no."

"You have to understand—"

"Wait," Melissa said. "How long was I here?"

"We didn't know what to do," Celeste said. "And back then, we had things we didn't want people to see. We couldn't just invite people here, into that, which we needed, and even after you fell asleep, to take you somewhere, to travel, that wouldn't have been easy."

"What are you talking about?" Melissa said.

"You slept and slept," Ron said, "for days, but you woke up sometimes—"

"Sometimes you walked, or crawled around. You folded the towels, arranged things. You loved to straighten anything. You'd walk to the window and stand sideways if there were birds outside. The thing of it was, you were getting better, most of the time."

"She was here for days?" Benjamin said.

"Well, we had to think about what to do. We had the

whole crop just harvested, the plants drying in the barn, and all of that was illegal, then."

"And you were getting better," Celeste said, looking at Melissa. "Your skin, your face got worse, though. We couldn't get it clean, it was like a kind of—what, a shadow—where it was dark or dim, like a scribbling over it, but sometimes it would shift and we could see through it. It wore down, some. Thinned out."

"It wasn't even really on your skin, it was like above your face, somehow. And we thought you could, you would start to talk, once that started thinning out, and then you'd tell us who you were, what to do."

"But you didn't talk, really. All the hissing and the noises you made, and the only real word was a name, but even then we weren't sure."

"Derek?" Melissa said.

"Something like that," Ron said.

"It got to where you'd been here for whatever reason for those days," Celeste said, "and we hadn't told anyone and were afraid to tell someone after that time. We didn't want to be blamed or suspected of something, you know—the time to tell, to report it, was kind of past. And we were afraid of how you were, how you'd lapse into that crawling and then seem normal again, how you weren't talking—"

"We thought we'd get blamed for how you were," Ron

said, "even though you were that way when you came to us. We even tried to let you go, turn you loose——"

Celeste reached out, then, and touched her husband's shoulder.

"The thing is," Ron said. "The thing of it was, we really didn't know what to do. And we thought, well, we'd just take you a couple towns over, to White Salmon, and maybe let you out there——"

"We talked about leaving you somewhere safe," Celeste said. "Not just out on the street or at night or something."

"But we couldn't do it," Ron said.

"It felt wrong," Celeste said. "We drove around and around with you in the backseat bellowing and moaning like you did, slapping at the windows; and finally we came back here and hid everything away, the whole crop, and then we called."

"By then," Melissa said, "you'd heard about the missing girl, Helen Hanson, about me?"

"But we didn't know right away," Ron said.

"And you're fine, now, aren't you?" Celeste said. "If you look back at it, the whole story, a lot didn't make sense. We were the people who helped. Your father, too—you, sir— what you said didn't really make sense, either."

"Wait," Melissa said.

"We wondered about that," Celeste said, "how you said

you were all the way, so far away camping and then she showed up here, farther than anyone could really walk. And then we thought maybe we were helping, to keep the girl safe—"

"This isn't about him," Melissa said.

"You came to us," Ron said. "We didn't take you from anyplace. We weren't looking for you or tricking you into coming here. We were trying to help. We didn't know what to do. It was something more than we could handle or understand. I mean, that whole time you never talked, never walked on your legs, never told us anything."

"In her sleep she talked," Celeste said. "But it didn't make sense. Mixed up, garbled. Maybe a name, everything so fast, like you were asleep and upset at the same time."

"Like something was after you," Ron said.

"You couldn't keep a blanket on top of you. You'd just kick it off."

"So why," Melissa said, "why did you tell them you knew who I was, that you knew I was missing?"

"It was easiest," Celeste said. "They acted like we would have, like we should have known, so we went along with that. We didn't want any trouble."

"And why'd you call the police, after all that time?"

"We didn't know what to do," Ron said. "And we were

a little frightened at what was happening. You didn't seem to be getting better the way we thought you should, even after we thought you were, then you never started talking or anything."

"We didn't do anything wrong," Celeste said.

"We didn't really do anything except help you," Ron said.

. . .

JOHNSON HAD SETTLED down, sleeping in the back. Benjamin sat next to Melissa, up front, as she drove. The two didn't speak until they'd retraced their path along the gravel road and were on the highway, following the winding river, heading south.

"They seemed kind of relieved," she said, "to be talking about it all. Did you feel that?"

"They were hoping we were about to leave and we wouldn't come back." Benjamin picked up the flashlight, rolling near his feet, and returned it to the glove compartment. "And why'd you say you were Helen?"

"Did that bother you?"

"No," he said. "It was surprising, is all."

"It did bother you."

"I guess so. A little."

"Well," Melissa said, "if I'd tried to explain who I actually am and why I was there—that would've slowed everything down, confused it, and we might never have gotten where we needed to go. Mostly I wanted to startle them a little, to put them on the defensive, so they would talk."

"They were definitely startled."

"It worked. I mean, I believe what they said, that they told us everything they could."

"I wish they'd said all that when it happened. It might have changed how everything went, between me and Helen."

"Did she ever say anything about them? About what happened, there?"

"I don't know," he said. "Not to me. I'm pretty sure she doesn't remember."

. . .

THEY REACHED THE Columbia, turned west, toward White Salmon, then took the bridge across to Hood River. The rain had eased, the moon sliding along in the black water, far below.

"When I think about what happened," Melissa said, "where Helen went, mostly it's about her brother, how she was trying to find her brother."

"Derek."

"Yes. Do you think she ever found him? Wherever she went?"

"He died," Benjamin said. "I don't think—"

"She never said anything about it?"

"I don't know," he said. "Not to me."

Melissa accelerated up the ramp, onto the interstate. Semitrailers shuddered past, to the left, the town of Hood River already behind them. Johnson snored from the backseat.

"The thing of it is," Melissa said, "I can't remember the last thing I said to Janice, even the last thing we were talking about. It was so sudden."

She glanced over at Benjamin, then stared out the window again.

A barge slid along the wide black river.

"We'd found the perfect house," she said. "It was way out a back road, halfway to the coast. Near a town called Elsie? She'd climbed a phone pole and been listening in on a line and heard a guy talking about it, this little hidden house. So we found it. We could've lived there a long time—we'd set up an alarm, far down the dirt road, but a calendar on the refrigerator marked out when he'd be there, too."

"When was this?"

"Three years ago. I told you that, before."

"Sorry."

The Bonneville Dam glowed on the right, its long curved walls white beneath the lights.

"The owner lived in Texas," Melissa said, "and this cabin was half dug into a hillside, all stocked with food and things for the end of the world or something. Peaches in cans, that sweet syrup. A generator that we didn't use—there was electricity, but we detached the meter, wired around it. There was solar, hot water. Everything. We had the best times, there. Read books, gave each other matching stick-and-poke tattoos—"

"The one on your neck?"

"Yes," she said. "And we read aloud to each other. *The Outsiders*, *Wuthering Heights*, *Lonesome Dove*. There were all kinds of books there, and a record player, too. Only classical music, but I got to like it because that's what those days sounded like, hardly any words at all. If only things could've stayed like that, but then there was the fire." She paused, checking the rearview mirror. "I left a propane tank next to the stove. I thought she got out, ahead of me, but she was inside searching for me—it was Johnson who got out first, who ran out ahead."

Before long, the lights of Portland on the horizon, radiating into the night sky.

11/3/2018 4:47 PM Transcription of Audio Capture

Benjamin: Helen, hello. I know you're busy. I'm
fine, here, pretty much the same. I'm still wondering when you might visit me, and whether you've
remembered anything more. I wonder about all that
time you were lost and then also after you were
found.

+

And what happened at the hospital? Did you go to a
hospital? I don't know. Was there something about
your skin, some kind of shadow on your skin? Or
something about your eyes?

+

You don't have to answer any of that. It is what
I'm wondering, though, and now that I've said it I
can't take it back.

+

You asked if I had more things, more of your things

from back then. I do—just a small box, some of the clothes you left and never retrieved, a science textbook, a pack of cards. I've moved with that box, carried it with me from place to place. I can show it to you, when you come. For now, here's one thing—from this notebook that's mostly empty, half the pages torn out, only a little bit of your writing.

+

Facsimile

TO	FROM
COMPANY	COMPANY
FAX (650) 234-2920	FAX (503) 517-7659
SUBJECT	DATE 11.3.2018 5:26 PM

~~Vhrlek~~

Derek

Passersthrough

farSeeing

The house—the murder house, the hell house—had disappeared.

All that remained was a square hole with one sloping edge, a yellow bulldozer in the bottom, surrounded by white gravel. A piece of plywood leaned against the fence; it had been spray-painted with numbers, a changed address: 7742, no longer 7734.

Benjamin glanced around—no neighbors' faces in windows, no cars driving by—then walked down the slope, gravel beneath his feet. The bulldozer's tracks had corrugated the stones and mud; the walls of earth around him had been pounded flat. Even the foundation was gone, as if no part of the house and what had happened here could be allowed to remain.

When he looked up from the bottom of the excavation,

it was as if he was at the bottom of a deep pool, gazing through the surface of the water at the sky.

Days had passed. No messages from Helen, no sign of Melissa.

Slowly, he walked up the slanting earth, stamping his boots in the street, the mud from his soles, and headed for home.

. . .

JAVIER WAS OUT on the sidewalk, trying to do tricks on his skateboard. The board flipped, landed upside down on the grass just as Benjamin approached.

"Sorry." The boy wore an orange windbreaker, gray sweatpants with torn knees; his hair looked like he'd cut it himself, the sides shaved.

"Sorry for what?"

"It's your lawn."

"You're not hurting anything." Benjamin walked past, then turned and stepped toward Javier. "Have you seen anyone?"

"Who?"

"Has anyone come by my house, anyone looking for me?"

"I don't know." The boy's jacket was too large; arms at his sides, the tips of his fingers barely peeked out of the cuffs. "I wasn't watching it."

"What happened to your hair?"

"It's a mohawk," Javier said, reaching up to touch it. "My mom did it."

"That's how you wanted it?"

"Yes."

"Listen," Benjamin said, as the boy began to turn away. "I know, I never showed you how to sharpen knives."

"That's okay."

"Someone didn't like it, the idea of me teaching you."

Javier licked his chapped lips. "I forgot about it."

"Is your mother home?" Benjamin said.

"Yes." The boy checked behind him, over his shoulder.

"Maybe sometime when she's not, you could just bring the knife over, and I can show you."

With one foot, Javier was pushing the skateboard back and forth on the sidewalk; its wheels made a squeaky, gritty sound.

"Tomorrow?" he said.

"Okay," Benjamin said. "I'll have things ready."

Facsimile

TO B	FROM Helen
COMPANY	COMPANY
FAX (503) 517-7659	FAX (650) 234-2920
SUBJECT	DATE 11.6.2018 12:37 PM

Still so busy, here. Thank you for your last message. I'd like to see that box, the notebook and everything. I've been looking at plane tickets, hoping to get up there to see you soon. Next weekend, it's Shauna's birthday, so there's a lot to do for that.

Where are you coming up with all these questions?

I know that Mom took me out of the hospital before they wanted, and later they wanted to examine me but she wouldn't let them. She's probably the only person who could answer some of these questions, and she's gone.

Not that she would ever really talk about it when she was alive.

The other day I tied all the knots you taught me, to see if I still could. It was like my fingers still knew the way to go.

End

In the basement, that afternoon, Benjamin found his whetstone and set it aside. Next, he straightened his tools, their outlines drawn on the pegboard, and began organizing all the various fasteners and hardware. Belts, screws, nails, plastic anchors. Sandpaper of various grades, filed away. Duct tape, electrical tape, Teflon tape. Measuring tapes of all shapes and sizes.

Upstairs in the kitchen, the phone began ringing. He dropped the brass hinges in their drawer and clattered upward, afraid he wouldn't get there in time.

"Hello?"

"Catch your breath."

"Helen?"

"It's Melissa. Are you ready to get going?"

"Now? Where?"

"I'm out in your car, just down the street, waiting."

"Right now?"

"A misadventure," she said.

He looked out the window at the gray sky, the sequoia's branches rising and falling in the wind.

"I thought we were helping each other," she said. "I've packed your things."

Benjamin pressed his hand against the cold window as Melissa drove.

She was wearing her overalls again, hiking boots he hadn't seen before, a thick red sweater that was unraveling along her left shoulder. Her hair was still cut short, of course; she looked halfway between her impersonation of Helen and how she usually did.

His metal camping stove rested in the backseat; behind that, in the space near the hatchback, two bulging frame packs jutted up.

"How long have you had my car?" he said.

"A couple days," she said. "You didn't miss it, did you?"

"You could ask."

"Aren't we beyond that, now?"

They stopped at a light. A bicycle, painted completely

white, was chained to a street sign, a dried-out bouquet of flowers leaning against its wheel.

. . .

OUT PAST RHODODENDRON and Zigzag, climbing toward the mountain, shrouded in clouds. The sharp white tops of the pines, a rind of dirty snow along the edge of the road.

Benjamin flipped down the visor, looked into the mirror there; he'd stopped shaving because of the scab, where the dog had bitten him, and now his beard wasn't growing back along the bite. It emphasized the scar, rather than hiding it.

"Where's the dog?" he said.

They climbed a long curve, a sheer cliff to the right; the sharp points of treetops jutted up from below.

"Johnson?" Melissa said. "He's with Cisco—they're keeping each other company, wherever they are—"

As she turned her head to look at him, all at once the car lurched sideways, skidded, slammed into something, the gray sky gone.

Dark fur pressed against the windshield, the tan and white of the individual hairs. The glass spidered out, cracking as the animal slid off to the side—then the body was up again and still moving, still hobbling with its head at an angle; careening, it crashed out across the edge of the highway, across the shoulder and, falling down the embankment, disappeared—

—and then visible again, collapsing through the underbrush, swallowed up.

Everything was still. There were no other cars, it seemed. No one around. Melissa leaned forward, squinting low beneath the cracks in the windshield.

"Doe and a fawn. Poor little guy." She leaned back, accelerated, then turned the car left, almost a U-turn, up the edge of the runaway truck ramp; she reversed, then shifted forward again, back the way they'd come.

"What are you doing?" he said.

Descending, she watched carefully out the side window, staring into the underbrush.

"Happened so fast. Where were we? Tell me if you see any blood on the road, any marks, anything—oh, here we go—"

She swung the car to the left again, across the lane and the shoulder, clattering down the embankment, finally sliding to a halt in a gap between bushes.

"Wait here," she said, already leaping out, her door left open and the hatchback up behind them, too, where she was pulling things loose.

Benjamin opened his door, climbed out just in time to see her running away down the slope carrying a coil of dark rope and a knife in a leather sheath. She disappeared into a thicket, and for a moment he could trace where she was by the branches' trembling. Then the bushes settled and he could no longer tell where she was.

"Melissa?" he called, but there was no answer. He took two steps down the slope, in the direction she'd gone, then turned back to the car. She'd said to wait.

He untied, tightened, retied the laces on his boots. His fingers wouldn't settle.

And then a cry rose up from below, shrill and sudden against the silence, and was just as suddenly gone. A car passed behind him, up on the highway, beyond where he could see. Birds shot black from the treetops.

"Melissa?"

He was halfway down the slope when she emerged from the underbrush, the knife in her hand. Bending down, she wiped its blade on the long grass, then her pant leg, before sliding it back into its sheath. She squinted up toward him, smiling as she approached.

"What happened?" he said.

"I'll show you." There was blood bright on her pants, on the cuffs of her shirt. "Let's get our things."

At the car, Melissa handed Benjamin the smaller of the two packs and shouldered the larger one. She took the camping stove in one hand, then circled the car, closing the doors and locking it before glancing up toward the highway.

"This'll be all right, here," she said. "I don't think anyone could see it from the highway. Follow me." She started down the slope, toward the bushes again. "That pack feel all right?"

Closer to the highway, the long grass was tangled with plastic bags, crushed cans, trash thrown from cars, but as they went deeper the ground was clear. They entered the bushes, heading into the underbrush, his pack catching on branches, turning him sideways. Melissa helped unsnag him.

After twenty or thirty feet, they came to a clearing, and there on the ground rested the small deer, its throat cut, its head bent back. One side of its skull was crushed in, where it had hit the car, the eye gone.

"Yearling," Melissa said. "Or not quite."

She slipped her pack from her shoulders, dropping it with a heavy clatter, then took out the knife again. Kneeling, she rolled the deer onto its back, held out the skin along the stomach, and began cutting a straight line up toward the head, pulling the edges of the skin as she went.

"Look here," she said, "how the ribs are all broken—can't believe the stomach's still intact. Broken forelegs, too; unbelievable he made it this far."

Benjamin heard something, a cracking in the thicket behind him, but when he turned nothing was there. Silence; only the sound of his breathing, and Melissa, and the cutting of the knife through the skin. Now the skin was pulled up to the neck, open like a cardigan sweater, the chest white with fat and muscle. Melissa reached into the deer's neck to take hold of the esophagus, then cut it in two; next, still holding the loose end, she backed up, pulling the guts out until they rested on the ground between her feet.

"Can you find a stick for me," she said, looking up at him, "a thick branch? A couple feet, forked on both ends if you can find one."

Once he had, she pierced the tendons above the back knees, inserted the stick, and tied knots there, holding the legs wide. Coiling the loose end of the rope, she threw it over a tree branch; with Benjamin's help she pulled until the deer was hanging, its front hooves grazing the ground, its broken head twisting. Blood dripped black against the pale dried leaves.

Knife in hand again, Melissa began to cut the skin loose, pulling it down the back of the deer's body.

"No," she said, when Benjamin reached to help. "No reason for you to get bloody, too. In my pack, though, can you get, in the top compartment there, there's some plastic bags, trash bags. Grab one for me?"

When he stood and turned again, the deer's skin was all inside out and glistening with fat, pulled down and hanging over the deer's head like a ragged white skirt. Melissa drew the tip of her knife along the backbone, her free hand digging a long strip of muscle free. She turned, and he held open the mouth of the bag so she could slip in the meat, a piece the size and shape of a small trout; next, she cut a strip from the other side of the backbone and dropped it, red and dripping, into the bag as well.

"Backstraps," she said. "Dinner. Maybe breakfast, as well."

As she wiped her hands and knife clean, Benjamin tied off the top of the bag.

"Here," she said, "take out that water bottle, pour a little on my hands."

Next, she pulled the rope so the deer's carcass swung higher in the air. She tied off the end, and cut the rope, attached the coil to her pack atop the folded blue tarp.

"This isn't how I wanted to start out," she said. "But we have to trust it. And I guess we're better provisioned. Let's go."

"Should I carry this bag of meat?"

"Here, I'll attach it to your pack. We might have to trade off, carrying this stove."

As she headed off through the trees, leading the way, the stove's metal sides bent and echoed slightly, slapping her thigh with a musical sound.

Hurrying after her, Benjamin looked back once at the deer's carcass, twisting slightly, glowing white against the green of the trees. It seemed to float there, rather than hang.

. . .

THE TRAILS THEY followed were made by animals, not people.

At first Benjamin had worried about being left behind, but as he fell into a rhythm he remembered how much he'd always liked this feeling, walking deeper, the leaves and feathery branches of a tight path welcoming him, urging him along. Moss grew bright underfoot, ferns in the crooks of branches above. Sunlight slanted through, winked away.

"How," he said, "how'd you learn to do all that? With the deer, I mean."

"My sister taught me," Melissa said. "Janice, she could do anything."

The air turned colder in the shadows. They crossed a creek, around a bend, then passed a dirty, abandoned couch, half burned, embroidered with flowers, pocked with bullet holes. Benjamin shifted the weight on his back; the gaps between trees opened and closed as he walked, shapes shifting in his peripheral vision.

"You think someone's following us?"

"No." Melissa turned, a line of dried blood marking her jaw; she unscrewed the lid from a water bottle, took a drink, handed it to him. "How you doing? You tired?"

"I don't know," he said. "I guess I forgot to be tired."

Unbuckling her pack, she swung it around, set it down, and began rummaging through it. She turned, after a moment, with something black in her hand. It was a mask—the kind used for sleeping, for travel, with an elastic strap. She fit it over her head; on the black fabric of the mask, two shiny golden eyes had been painted, thick lashes around them.

"I thought maybe I'd try to walk like this," she said, "and you could follow me, and then we'd just see where we end up."

When he didn't answer, she pushed the mask up on her forehead, so it was as if she had four eyes, all staring at him.

"Can we just try it?" she said. "Isn't this how it works?"

Overhead, a squirrel leapt from one tree to another. Branches shook, settled.

"It's different," he said. "You're not my daughter. It's a different time, different state, different mountain, everything."

"But we're the only people here. And here we are."

Benjamin looked up through the trees' branches, at the gray sky, then down at Melissa. She slid the mask over her eyes again.

"We need the rope," he said, "to tie it to your belt, so I can hang on, and follow."

Once the rope was attached, they set out again. Melissa stumbled on a root, caught herself, a clatter of pans in her pack. Benjamin kept the rope almost taut, holding her back before she ran into a tree.

"Aren't you supposed to warn me?" She lurched sideways, and he followed.

"I don't know," he said. "I really can't remember, but I don't think there were directions or even talking. I think it should be silent."

Slowly they wandered, Melissa's hands out in front of her. She whispered to herself, words he couldn't hear. Next she veered to the left, into some brush, and before he could pull her back the rope was so snarled and tangled he had to tell her to stop.

"We're getting nowhere," she said, her eyes uncovered now. "Let's switch places. Maybe it should be you."

. . .

THE BLACKNESS WAS nearly complete, once the mask was over his eyes, almost no light around the edge. His balance shifted. He took a step, stopped, then began again.

"Take it slow," Melissa said.

"I think I need more slack in the rope," he said, "so I can't feel you're there."

He walked haltingly through the darkness, expecting to run into a tree or collapse into bushes, to trip on a rock or root. Above, around him, the birds were calling, warning each other. The cold wind ruffled his whiskers, chapped his lips. His boots scuffed along.

"When people are lost in the wilderness," Melissa said, "a right-handed person will veer and wander to the right, and a left-handed one will—"

"I think no talking," he said, standing still, turning toward where he felt she was. "It should be silent, if there's any chance."

AND THEN THROUGH the silence he went, the darkness like velvet, his pack gradually weightless, buoyant so he could hardly feel the ground, no friction; it was no longer as if a rope was attached behind him, but rather as if a line was attached out in front, gently pulling him along, guiding his way.

Or as if he were standing still and an unseen landscape was slipping around him.

He kept on, the wind in his ears a soft voice, voices, his feet certain.

"OKAY," HE SAID. "I think this is where we should stop."

"I can talk now?"

Benjamin pulled off the mask; the light was sharp in his eyes, though the day had grown dim. He stood in a small clearing, surrounded by pines.

"You found it." Melissa took off her pack, leaned it against a tree.

Off to one side of the clearing, then, he saw the lean-to, its blue tarp bright against the tree trunks.

"I can't believe you found it," she said.

"What is this?" Benjamin said, stepping closer, reaching

out to touch the tarp, so new its creases still showed; the ropes lashing it together also looked new.

"We built it," she said. "Me and Cisco. But this isn't where it was."

"This isn't where you built it?"

"Here, go inside. Is this how it looked, more or less?"

Benjamin bent down, crawled inside, across a loose sleeping pad, a tangled down sleeping bag. Deeper, there was a red plastic box that held a signal mirror, a whistle, and a headlamp. Fishing line coiled inside a shoe polish tin, hooks nestled together.

Melissa bent down, watching him. "You just went and went," she said. "As if you could see perfectly, or like you were sleepwalking. You really couldn't see?"

"No," he said.

"Amazing. And how did it feel?"

"I was just following along," he said. "Being pulled along."

"So, what do you think—the rice cakes, those dried fish, are they like the ones you had?"

"Close enough."

"What does that mean?"

"They're the same kind of fish, I think."

"What about these protein bars?"

"It was just granola bars," he said. "I don't think you

could buy this kind of thing, back then. Why's there an extra sleeping bag?"

"Someone might need it, sometime," she said. "You hungry? It's getting dark. Let's start a fire."

.   .   .

BENJAMIN WATCHED AS Melissa undid her necklace, struck the stone so sparks rained down into the tinder.

"Faro and flint," she said. "Works when it's wet, too."

"We could just use the stove," he said. "You carried it all this way."

"Better to save the fuel," she said. "Keep the stove for the lean-to, any passersthrough that might find it—"

"It's just," he said. "It's a lot, this is a lot. You built this, when?"

"Last week."

"And we happened to crash right there, and here we are?"

"Yes—but we didn't build it, here. We were far from here." She leaned forward on her knees, blew on the tinder; flames leapt up, into the tepee she'd built of kindling. "Tell me," she said. "What is a passerthrough?"

"They're just something we used to talk about, me and Helen."

"Like a through-hiker, or something else?"

"Maybe something else?" Benjamin looked over at the shadowy lean-to, then stared into the sky, the moon's hazy glow. "She used to say they were caught between places, passersthrough, between someplace and someplace else."

"And they took the things from the lean-to?"

"Someone did. Anyone could have."

"Between someplace and someplace else," Melissa said. "Maybe we're passersthrough, right now."

They set to building up the logs, then sat down to watch the fire, stretching forward to make adjustments, to be sure it would catch. The flames rose up, red and orange, cinders drifting, gone to ash.

"All of this, my sister taught me," Melissa said. "She could do anything, in the woods, in the city. She could get into buildings from tunnels beneath the street, she could stay right in your blind spot, she could follow a person like that." Standing, Melissa stepped into the shadows, dragged more wood to the fireside. "She was the best. So funny. You know what her favorite word was? 'Bluster.' That was like her mantra—she said you had to keep moving forward, you never wanted someone to even have time to draw a breath to say something, to question you."

"She was older?"

"A couple years."

"Everyone should have a big sister," he said.

"Did you?"

"No," he said. "I was an only child."

The shadows surrounding them crept closer, leapt away as they watched the flames.

"What about your parents?" he said.

"My parents?" Melissa laughed, spat over her shoulder. "I have no idea—never met them, don't plan to. We were foster kids, that's how it was. That's when I met her."

"So you weren't really sisters," he said. "Not biologically, I mean."

"We were sisters," she said.

. . .

THEY ROASTED THE venison, on spits of green branches, ate it with dough Melissa had wrapped around sticks.

"No one's ever eaten more roadkill than me." She sat across from Benjamin, firelight flickering in her face. "And deer's the best."

"What's the worst?"

"Nutria, probably." She set her stick down, then stood, disappeared into the darkness; after a moment she returned with an armful of wood.

"After how things went with the blindfold," she said, "I think maybe it should be you who sleeps in the lean-to."

"You can sleep there, too. There's room."

"I'll be right over here. I'll tie my hammock between those trees."

They both stared into the flames, leaping and falling.

"Did you hear something?" he said.

"It's just the fire."

He felt the warmth on the soles of his feet, the cold pressing at his back. Sparks rose up, burned to ashes, drifted gray against the black sky. And then he heard breathing, something behind him, a chuffing breath that stopped, then started again.

A crashing in the bushes.

Melissa leapt to her feet, a flashlight shining from her hand. Silence. He turned, watching the light, the tree trunks and the shadows between them. Then: two eyes. Twenty feet away, glowing in the underbrush.

"A deer," Melissa said. "It's only a deer."

At the sound of her voice, the eyes disappeared, and there was a heavy, splintering sound, a flash of white tail.

. . .

FROM THE LEAN-TO, Benjamin could see Melissa's silhouette as she tied her hammock to one tree, stretched it to another. Her headlamp's beam sliced out into the tree trunks, down at her hands, at the knots she was tying, then over at him.

He switched on his own headlamp, holding it in his hand as he unrolled the foam sleeping pad and sleeping bag. Climbing in, stretching out, he shone his light along the plastic containers of food, the gallon of water, the stove. In the darkness, he heard the fire, its logs collapsing in on themselves.

A little later, off in the trees, the breathing again.

He called: "Melissa?"

"Right here. What is it?"

"I think it's the deer, out there," he said. "It's the mother of the one we hit, that we ate."

"What?"

"I can feel it," he said. "She's been following us."

"I doubt that very much," Melissa said. "Go to sleep. And even if it is a deer—what's it going to do?"

HE AWAKENED, THE skin of his face cold. The fire had burned out, every coal. He heard nothing, no breathing, no wind. Next to him, though, lying flat, was the shape of a person. When he saw the edge of the lean-to, he knew it was Helen.

No, it was not Helen. It was Melissa. Slowly, he reached out to touch her shoulder, but when he did she crumpled away. Beneath his hand was only his down jacket, collapsed into nothing.

He lay awake—listening, his heart slowing as he thought of how it felt to walk blindfolded, through that soft blackness to this place.

SOMETHING WAS GLOWING, when he next awakened, something round, far across the clearing from the lean-to. Something on the ground. Benjamin unzipped his sleeping bag, sat up, found his glasses. Their frames were cold against his ears, his nose.

It was the moon—he saw it in the sky, now, as he leaned out from under the tarp—and it was also on the ground, in the water, the reflection of the moon in water. A pond, a small lake.

He kicked his legs free, dug out his pants, stood up outside the lean-to.

"Melissa?"

There was no answer.

He stepped toward where the fire had burned, where the hammock had hung, but there were no coals, no ashes, no hammock. Melissa was not here.

He walked to the edge of the water, so dark with the moon out in the middle, his own black reflection. And then the clouds slid across the moon, and he could see through the water's surface, the white shapes on the bottom. Antlers? Bones? In the shallows, their sharp shapes blurring, fading as the depths slanted away from him.

Silence. A ripple along the shore.

A white bone shifted, and another. Movement in the depths. He leaned closer. Was that a hand? A small, pale hand, lifting a thin, sharp bone aside. And then another hand, and a third and a fourth. Four hands, not so pale as the bones, lifting and settling the bones.

A face? A small face looked up at him, ten feet or more beneath the surface. And then another, two faces, rising, their bodies dark, and then their bare feet visible, deeper.

He stepped back, watching.

The crowns of their heads, dark hair slick, first broke the water's surface, and next their faces. Children. They paused, five feet offshore, with the dark water a line around their necks. For a moment, all was silent.

Benjamin checked his watch, but his watch was not on

his wrist. He looked at his hands, counted his fingers. He closed his eyes, opened them again. Hopped into the air, and landed heavily, did not float or levitate.

"Hi," said the smaller child, a boy, waving his pale hand above the surface of the water. "I saw you, before. I saw you when you came to our house and walked around and even down in the basement."

"Do you think you're dreaming?" the other child said. She was a girl, the larger child. "Well, you're not."

"You're doing great, though." The boy's voice was pitched even higher than the girl's. "You're doing really good."

Slowly, the children continued to surface, splashing forward until they stood on shore, next to Benjamin in the moonlight. They were not wet, he realized, their hair already dry, their dirty clothes also dry, and torn. A dark stain marked the girl's blouse, spreading across her chest as she stood there, looking up at him. The boy's head angled to one side, his ear almost touching his shoulder; there was a black line, a deep cut along the side of his neck.

"Are you going to say anything?" the boy said.

"What's happening?" Benjamin said.

"You seem frightened." The girl laughed, her eyes as black as her shining hair. "How could we ever do you any harm?"

"I don't know," he said. "Where is this? Where were you?"

"It has no name, really," the girl said. "Of course, Helen, Helen called it 'Sad Clown Lake.'"

"Helen?"

"Everyone," the girl said, "where we're from, everyone still talks about Helen, the way she was searching."

"Was she looking for her brother? Did she find him?"

"I never heard it that way," the boy said.

"But you knew, you know Helen?"

"We heard of her," the boy said.

"We're different from you," the girl said, "but you shouldn't think you're better than we are."

"No," Benjamin said. "I didn't—I didn't mean. I don't understand how it all works. Were you breathing, underwater?"

"Water?" the boy said.

Benjamin bent down, splashed his fingers in the wetness of the lake. He felt the children watching him, waiting, as if they expected something from him.

"Do you need my help?" he said.

"What kind of help?" the girl said.

"Are you looking for something? For someone? I don't know what I can do."

"Do you love us?" the boy said.

"It's a beautiful night," the girl said.

"It's literally starting to snow?" When the boy spoke,

black blood slipped from the wound in his neck. "This place, this place is pretty fun, I guess."

Thick white flakes disappeared into the dark water of the lake, settled along the shore, white on the children's dark heads. Benjamin felt the cold atop his feet, and realized that he wasn't wearing shoes or socks. The children were also barefoot, of course, and now they looked up at him, faintly smiling.

"It's really coming down!" the girl said.

"It could collect," the boy said. "It could pile up—"

"Accumulate," the girl said.

"It could literally accumulate," the boy said, "if we get lucky."

"We should get back now," said the girl. "We have other places to be."

"We're not even supposed to be here," the boy said.

"These bodies!" said the girl.

"Melissa brought you here," the boy said. "She's still your friend."

"Melissa?" Benjamin said. "You know her?"

"I like her dog," the boy said. "I tried and tried to pet him."

"Her dog was here?"

"Yes," the girl said. "With that Francisco. You know that boy?"

"He's funny!" the boy said. "His freckles!"

"He sure wanted to get away from here," the girl said. "He was scared of us, if you can believe that."

"I only wanted to pet that dog," the boy said. "But he was so skittery."

"Skittish," the girl said.

"They were where?" Benjamin said. "Where are they now?"

"Gone, now," the boy said.

The boy was looking past Benjamin, into the black shadows beneath the trees. Benjamin turned; no one was there, no one he could see.

"We've watched Melissa," the girl said. "We like her. It's a nice name, too."

"It's actually a kind of plant," the boy said. "Or a flower?"

"An herb," the girl said. "There used to be a Melissa at my school, but that's not the same Melissa."

"Have you ever talked to her?" Benjamin said.

"No," the girl said. "We heard Janice, though, we talked to Janice, or she talked to us. She said she doesn't blame Melissa."

"She could literally barely talk!" the boy said. "She's all burned up, like her face and her arm."

"She talked just fine," the girl said. "No one talks the same. There's no right way to talk."

The boy shook his head, and it tilted up so far it seemed it might detach from his body. He pushed it back with his hand and walked away, already up to his waist in the water, submerging, his head going last.

"Goodbye, Benjamin," the girl said. "It's time for everyone to sleep."

"Where do you sleep?"

"Everywhere."

"Where's your mother?"

"Somewhere else."

Turning, she followed the boy, the dark water closing over her legs, her waist, her shoulders, ripples sent out from her in all directions. And then the lake went still as her head slipped under. Both children descended; it was as if they were walking down stairs, away from him, their heads growing smaller, fading to nothing, their white hands going last.

Still, the snow. His breathing, only. Behind him, he was relieved to see the lean-to, and he shuffled to it, found his socks and boots; he pulled them on, stood again.

"Melissa?"

He walked a loose, oblong spiral, out away from the lake, calling her name, checking back for his footprints in the snow, so he would not get lost. In the trees, the ground was bare, and he paused, nervous about losing his way if he could not follow his footprints back. Standing still, he heard a step, a breath against the cold darkness.

"Are you there?" he said.

Nothing. He turned slowly, his body tense. Silhouettes, shadows. And then movement, a shift to his left, the breathing coming hard, a grunting sound like a warning.

It was the deer, the mother deer. Its two eyes collected the only light in the thicket. Ten feet away, it stood perfectly still, watching him.

"Can you speak?" Benjamin said. "I'm sorry."

At his words the deer leapt away, out of the trees, into the snow, which muffled all sound.

He wandered the edge of the tree line until he found his footprints, half filled with snow, and followed them back to the lean-to. Shivering, he climbed back into his sleeping bag.

Silence.

The falling snow, the still black water, the lake bed sharp with bones.

IT WAS AS if something or someone had gently touched his face—a hand? A deer's nose?—but he opened his eyes to brightness and he was alone.

All around the lean-to, white. Six inches of snow. The sky bright blue.

Benjamin sat up, squinted across the clearing. There was no lake, unless it had frozen, been snowed over; even then, the trees were too close, there was no room for the lake. His footprints from last night, were they there? It was impossible to know.

"This was not in the forecast," Melissa was saying, stamping her feet, coming closer. "You all right? It's afternoon. Almost two." She bent down, looked in at him. "I kept checking on you—you were sleeping and sleeping. I wish I could've understood what you were talking about, and it was impossible to wake you up."

Benjamin put on his socks and boots, his jacket. His skin felt tight, and his head ached. Sunlight caught in icicles, hanging from the branches all around. He stuffed his sleeping bag into its sack, reached out for his pack.

"Let's leave all that here," Melissa said.

Standing, he shuffled out across the snow, then bent down and swept it away, revealing the bare ground.

"What are you doing?"

"I saw those children," he said.

"Who?"

"Those dead children. They came out of the lake."

Melissa stepped closer.

"It was right here," he said. "The lake. And they came up out of it, and their clothes were dry. The boy's neck was cut so his head—"

"This was last night?" Melissa said. "Ben, what?"

"Did you wake up in the night and I was gone?"

"No," she said. "I slept until this morning. And you were still asleep, right here, and you've been sleeping so hard—I reached in, shook you, but you didn't wake up."

"These were the children from the house," he said. "Where you were. They said they liked you."

"They liked me?"

"You don't believe me?"

"I didn't say that."

"It wasn't a dream," he said. "The girl told me it wasn't— can that happen in a dream? Where someone tells you it's not a dream?"

"Ben, slow down."

"And I saw the deer, the mother deer, too. And that's when it started snowing. The children, they talked about Helen—they'd heard of her. She'd been there, where they are, and they heard she was looking for her brother."

Benjamin looked past Melissa, at the lean-to, then back at her face, the tip of her tongue pressed to the gap in her teeth.

"And then what?" she said.

"It's hard to remember everything," he said. "The way they talked, it was fast. Wait—Cisco! They'd seen Cisco."

"When?"

Benjamin paused at the eagerness, the anxiety in her voice. She leaned close.

"You lost Cisco?" he said. "Was he sleeping here, or where?"

"The children said he's there?"

"Not anymore," Benjamin said. "They said he was looking for you, but they didn't know where he was. And then, I don't know. They just went back into the lake, walking down and down until I couldn't see them anymore. But the children, they knew you. You know them?"

"I never saw them," she said. "They never spoke to me. I felt them, though, in the house. I knew they were there, and sometimes I spoke to them, to comfort them, so they'd know I knew, but they never showed themselves, never spoke to me."

. . .

BENJAMIN FOLLOWED MELISSA beneath the trees. As the sunlight grew stronger, snow sifted down from the branches above, sometimes collapsing in larger sections.

"You all right?" she said.

"Are we lost?"

"The children," she said, turning, waiting for him to catch up. "Did they know that they were dead?"

"We didn't talk about that," Benjamin said. "Not exactly. It was hard, the way the conversation was moving, to know how to talk to them."

As Melissa turned and he followed, again, he thought about how he'd traveled this same stretch of forest, yesterday; he tried to imagine how it would be, how it would look to see someone, him, walk easily between these trees, blindfolded. He had seen it, he had done it, and Helen had done it. And now Melissa was walking ahead in her jaunty way, her pack silent, no longer clattering, all the pots and pans left behind in the lean-to.

"Another thing they told me," he said, "the children—I forgot until now, but they told me that they talked to Janice, where they are."

"They talked to Janice?"

"They said she told them she doesn't blame you for what happened."

Melissa closed her eyes for a moment, paused, then began walking again. It seemed she was about to say something, but it was quite some time before she spoke.

"If that's right," she said, "I'd really like to believe it. I'd like to hear her say so."

"That's what they said," Benjamin said, hurrying to catch up. "They also said I was doing great."

"You are doing great," she said. "Come on, we're almost there."

. . .

THE DEER CARCASS had been torn down and dismembered, scattered along the ground. Melissa found the skin in the bushes, all ripped and full of holes.

"Thought I might tan this." She picked up one edge, dropped it again. "Guess not."

"What was it, do you think?"

"Cougar?" she said. "Whatever it was needed the meat more than we did."

Up on the highway, a snowplow clattered past, a white wave shooting along the top of the slope. Snow rested atop Benjamin's car, still parked where they'd left it. The fender, the front corner was dented in, the left headlight broken, dangling from a wire; the windshield was shattered, yet still in one piece.

"Wake up, Ben. You're home. Wake up."

He opened his eyes, wiped at his face, straightened himself in the passenger seat. It was dusk, rain drifting sideways, the streetlights flickering on. They were parked just down the street from his house.

She leaned across, the length of her body pressing against him, the campfire smell of her hair. She unlatched his door, pushed it open, then straightened up, her hands back on the wheel.

"Here," she said. "Take your raincoat. Get inside, out of this weather."

"You're taking my car?"

"Look at this windshield," she said. "I know someone who'll fix it."

He stood, pulling himself from the car, the rain cold on his bare head. Stepping onto the curb, he expected her to say something more, but the car was already rolling, the door slamming shut with the momentum. The one head-light swung brightly across the yards, reflected in the wet windows of his neighbors' houses; the brake lights flashed at the corner, red, and then she was gone.

. . .

IN THE KITCHEN, he switched on the lights, the thermo-stat, heard the furnace chuffing to life in the basement. He picked up the phone's handset from the wall and—uncertain whether to dial Helen, what to say—replaced it in the cradle.

His muddy footprints wandered from the back door, around the kitchen, leading to where he now stood.

All at once, when he unzipped his wet raincoat, the smell of smoke from the campfire and the roasting meat rose up, a greasy feeling on his skin.

. . .

IN THE GUEST bedroom, he took the old cardboard box from the closet's high shelf. The notebook slipped out, onto the floor, which revealed Helen's clothing, from when she was a girl, carefully folded and now unfolding as he lifted it from the box.

A bright green stocking cap, unraveled along the top. He set it on the pillow.

Below it, he spread her faded gray sweatshirt; one arm up as if waving, the other bent down at the elbow.

A pair of jeans, next, ragged at the hems; on the left knee, an iron-on patch, darker, peeled loose at a corner. The pockets of the jeans—empty.

And finally the moccasins, their stiff rawhide laces twisting loose, all the beads long gone. The moccasins had no soles, only leather, so Helen could walk through the forest without making a sound.

Benjamin: I went camping, and the lean-to, I woke up and the lake was there where there hadn't been a lake. The bones beneath the water and everything you said. I fell asleep and there was no lake, then I woke up and the lake was there. I wasn't dreaming, and these children came out of it. They were dead and they came out of the lake and told me they'd heard of you, of Derek.

+

I don't know. I don't understand what's happening and I'm afraid it's too much to tell you—I don't want you to stay away. And then it's also that you might understand this or recognize it more than I can.

+

Exhausted, he shed his clothes, piled them in the corner of his bedroom. He ran the bath, eased himself into the hot water.

The house was silent; all its usual sounds. The furnace, the creak of the timbers as the walls warmed up.

So tired, his body aching, he scrubbed at the black crescents of dirt in his fingernails. Were his fingers always this crooked, the skin of his hands always so papery? His knobby knees jutted, bent above the water's surface.

Leaning back, he dunked his head. Soap burned his eyes. He rubbed his face; pieces of scab came off against the washcloth. He shook water from one ear, then the other.

The next morning, the fax machine's tray was empty.

Benjamin stood in his kitchen, drinking coffee, looking out into the yard. Sunlight reflected off the ground beneath the window of the garage. Shards of glass; the window was broken.

Outside, he pushed open the gate and saw that the garage wasn't completely closed—a dark gap, just big enough for a person to crawl through, between the bottom of the garage door and the driveway. Stepping closer, he leaned down.

"Hello?"

After a moment, he gripped the bottom of the door and lifted it upward, ratcheting overhead.

Gray light eased in: his wood pile, scattered; gardening gloves like deflated hands around the floor; scrap wood strewn here and there. He picked up a 2x4 that seemed to have been gnawed, then stepped in further. Lengths of green hose, uncoiled and snaking down from the rafters. Red pieces of metal, underfoot—the runners of a sled, torn loose.

Nothing here was as he'd left it, and most everything was broken.

A voice, then, behind him:

"I saw him. He must've done it."

Benjamin turned; Javier stood there, at the end of the driveway, stepping closer, his sad mohawk flattened by the rain.

"Who?"

"That same boy. The one from the tree. Here." Javier pointed. "In your backyard, I mean. It was just weird. Maybe he was in your garage, or he came out of your garage, and he was trying to get into your house, I think, but he was like, I don't know, bouncing off it like he couldn't find the door."

"Slow down," Benjamin said.

"It was that same boy, but he was different, too. Like he wasn't walking—he was more like crawling, kind of, with his arms and legs straight." Javier bent down, to demonstrate. "Only he was fast, so fast like that. It wasn't like a boy or a person, so it was kind of scary."

"This was when?"

"Just before. When it was dark. I followed him." The boy looked out toward the street. "He went and went, and then he got into a truck."

Benjamin tossed the red metal sled runner aside, surprised to find it in his hand, and it clattered away across the concrete floor.

"Aren't you going to do something?" Javier unzipped his jacket, zipped it up again. "I mean, you know him, right?"

"You said he went away in a truck."

"No," Javier said. "He got into a truck—it was one of those camper trucks with a camper on the back, but it wasn't moving. It's parked."

. . .

THE RAIN HAD eased, turned to mist. They headed down the street, around puddles, Javier out ahead of Benjamin, pointing as he shouted back, his voice cracking:

"He was going zigzag, not straight. Like bumping into parked cars. It was darker, then, so he was going in and out of where I could see, in the streetlights. It wasn't really like he could tell I was following, I don't think. Sometimes he'd come back toward me and I'd hide, but then he'd get moving away again, and I'd follow."

"And he still wasn't walking on his feet?" Benjamin said.

"Not really. He was crawling, kind of, but upside down, too, facing up? See those bushes there, all messed up and broken? He got caught up in there and then he got loose and kept going this way. It was crazy—he'd hit his head against a tree or car and just keep on. Right up here's where he was."

They walked along a rutted, gravel alleyway, an unimproved side street choked with blackberries and ivy. They passed an abandoned shopping cart, a bent and rusted bicycle wheel.

"That's where he went," Javier said. "Into there."

As they turned a slight corner, Melissa's truck came into view; it was parked half in the underbrush, backed in, trees' branches pressing against the camper's side.

"Okay," Benjamin said. "Let's see."

"I'm late to school," Javier said, stepping back. "They probably already called my mom."

"Did you tell her, did you tell your mother about the boy?"

"I didn't tell anyone. No one was even awake." Javier was already turning.

Benjamin watched the boy run away, leaving him standing there alone. Rain misted down, collected in the gravel potholes.

Cautiously, then, he began to approach the truck. The wipers were up, across the windshield, paused in mid-swipe.

"Cisco?"

There was no answer, at first, and then, suddenly, barking—it echoed fiercely inside the camper.

Benjamin searched the ground to find something, a piece of wire to pick the lock; there was nothing.

And yet when he checked the doorknob, it was unlocked. Johnson's barking shifted to a growl.

"It's okay," Benjamin said. "You know me."

But when he swung the door open, Johnson bounded out with a garbled whine, knocking Benjamin to his knees, snarling away into the bushes.

In a moment, his black shape emerged, half a block away, limping slightly but not slowing as he disappeared around the corner.

Benjamin took hold of the truck's bumper and pulled himself to his feet. He crawled through the open door, inside.

The air was hot, damp, the light dim. Underfoot, papers, cords and ropes, pieces of computers, tangled clothing. Benjamin waded through, reached out, pushed the curtains aside so light slanted in; it was as if the truck had been in a storm at sea, a wild ride through a wilderness. Sweating, he stood still. Outside, a car passed, slowing to splash through the puddles, but didn't stop. Far away, someone shouted.

Closer—a raspy sound, in and out. Breathing.

There, in the space above the truck's cab, a tangle of blankets, a bumpy shape atop the foam rubber mattress. He stepped closer, pulled the blanket back.

A bare foot, covered in scratches, its sole blackened. Benjamin lifted the blanket, pushed it aside. Cisco. Wearing torn and dirty jeans; no shirt, and his skin shadowed with dirt or something more, different, a hovering scribble of darkness.

"Cisco," Benjamin said. "Don't worry, I'm here. It's me."

Cisco's face, it was also behind this shadow, his eyes closed. The breathing, the chest rising and falling. Heat rose from his body. Benjamin reached out, into the haziness, parting it with his fingers, and touched the boy's cheek.

Suddenly Cisco's eyes opened.

Was he awake? His eyes were only white, the pupils spun back, hidden. His breathing did not change, he did not seem to see Benjamin. His eyelids closed again. His chest rose and fell.

"It's okay," Benjamin said, leaning close.

He took hold of the boy's shoulder, and Cisco's hands came to life, rising slowly, slapping Benjamin away. The movements weren't violent, only the awkwardness of a sleeper not wishing to be awakened.

Outside, voices.

"I'll be back soon. Stay here." Benjamin covered the boy with the blanket. He pulled the curtains closed on his way back outside.

Climbing down, he closed and locked the door. As he did, a voice spoke, behind him.

"Is that your truck?"

Two women, one pushing a stroller, stood fifteen feet away.

"We live right there"—she pointed—"and we were about to call it in, get it towed. You can't just leave it here, have people living out here."

"I'm sorry," Benjamin said. "I'll move it. I'll do it today."

In the basement, he packed up the tools he'd need—wire, and wrenches, and pliers—into his metal toolbox. He tried to remember how it could be done; it wasn't complicated, in an old truck like Melissa's, just a matter of making a connection, the electricity jerking the starter, the engine firing and turning over.

And then a ringing, the telephone ringing. He spilled the toolbox, stumbled upstairs, but by the time he reached the kitchen, it was silent. He held the handset to his ear, then replaced it in its cradle.

He waited, but the phone did not ring again.

He hurried along the sidewalk, switching his metal toolbox from one hand to the other.

At the gravel side street, where Melissa's truck was parked, everything was still; nothing appeared to have changed. The camper's curtains were drawn.

Approaching, leaning close, he peered through the window, into the truck's cab: the usual assortment of hammers and maps, food wrappers.

He took a piece of wire from his toolbox, bent it; gently, he worked the wire between the edge of the door and the roof, slid it down, popped the lock. He tried to slow his breathing, to steady his hands as he slid inside, behind the wheel. He checked the ashtray, the glove compartment, under the seats and floor mats. No keys.

Taking out his largest screwdriver and the pry bar, he began to bend the plastic cladding away from the steering column.

Voices.

He quietly closed the door, leaned sideways, flat across the passenger seat, until it was silent again. And then, lying there on his side, he saw the silver edge of the key, right there in the ignition.

The engine kicked, it coughed, wouldn't quite turn all the way over. He tried again, and finally it caught, choking and stuttering.

The truck reluctantly eased out, the sound of gravel beneath the tires, the sharp scratching of the branches along the camper. Benjamin accelerated, lurching through potholes, out onto the street; the steering pulled to the right; he took it slow, his house only a few blocks away.

He parked in the driveway. The rain still fell, and no one was outside, but perhaps he should wait, leave Cisco in the truck, try to move him later, when it was darker? Of course, in the meantime the boy might awaken—and with that thought, Benjamin realized that he hadn't checked, that quite possibly the boy was no longer inside the camper, had escaped or wandered off.

He leapt out, rushed around back. The door of the camper was unlocked.

He turned the knob, pulled it open; moist heat spilled out around him. Stepping up, inside, he was careful of his footing, yet—despite how cluttered it had been earlier—the floor was now clear; as his eyes adjusted, he noticed the careful stacks of paper, off to one side, the folded clothing. The blankets were carefully folded, next to the pillow, and Cisco was not on the foam rubber mattress.

The boy, he sat perfectly still, at the table; lines of pens, pencils and screwdrivers were arrayed before him. Shirtless, barefoot, Cisco held a pencil in one hand, its point resting on a blank piece of paper.

"Hello," Benjamin said. "You did all this?"

The boy didn't answer, but it felt right, reassuring, to speak to him, to have it not be so silent, in that tight space. Benjamin stepped closer, leaned to look into Cisco's face. His eyes were closed; he appeared to be asleep, a gentle rise of his chest, skin clouded by the hovering scribble. Heat eased out from his body. Bruises on his shoulder, the side of his head—from colliding with the cars and trees, as Javier had described, or from whatever had happened, before that.

"You can't stay here," Benjamin said.

Cisco was surprisingly strong, his muscles clenched; it almost took the screwdriver to pry the pencil from his fingers.

"Muh," he said. "Muh, muh, muh," and then his lips hummed, and then he was silent.

His arms didn't want to straighten, then suddenly gave way, and his body turned heavy, floppy. Benjamin paused, sweating. He pulled the blanket loose, tried to wrap it around Cisco. The camper's door flapped open, cold air blowing in. The boy's skin was hot to the touch, the shadow slipping along its surface but not coming free.

"Can we walk?"

He took hold of Cisco under the arms, and lurched up, backward, so the boy fell against him. Almost as tall as Benjamin, his hot face smooth against Benjamin's neck. They struggled down to the driveway, Cisco getting free for a moment—trying to crawl, he didn't want to stand on his feet—yet somehow Benjamin got him up again.

He pulled Cisco's arms over his own shoulders, the boy's chest against his back; he walked that way, struggling, Cisco's feet dragging, his breathing raspy in Benjamin's ear, heat where their skin touched.

Squirrels chittered from atop the fence, switched their ragged tails back and forth. Wind blew the rain sideways.

Lurching through the gate, Benjamin managed to prop the back door open with a watering can, to get Cisco inside, finally into a chair, at the kitchen table.

Cisco continued his sleep, neck bent and head tilted over his shoulder. Slowly, slowly his balance shifted, and he slid from the chair, onto the floor, landing on his side, his arms and legs making crawling movements, the dirty soles of his feet going back and forth in the air.

Benjamin tried to calm, straighten him. The boy's skin was warm, still hot, his eyes clenched tight, his mouth panting.

"Wait. Stay here."

He rushed through the living room, the bedroom, and turned the spigot, began running a cold bath. Standing there, watching the water run, he forgot and then remembered the stopper. His knees ached as he bent down and fit it in, the water cold against his hands. He straightened up, hurried back to the kitchen.

Cisco still rested on the floor.

"Okay," Benjamin said. "Okay. Here."

He grasped the boy beneath his arms, dragged him half crawling through the doorway, past the bed, into the bathroom. And then stepped into the tub, wrenching his back as he hoisted Cisco, headfirst, the boy's legs flopping over, last, into the cold water.

Cisco didn't gasp or make any sound; his eyelids flickered, opened for only a second—pupils out to the sides of his head, barely visible—and then closed tight again. The shadows ran darker along the edges of his body, along the waterline, collecting in thicker stripes.

"That should cool you down," Benjamin said, pulling Cisco a little more upright, his face further from the water.

Stepping away, through the bedroom and into the living

room, he glimpsed Melissa's truck, through the window, and it took a moment before he remembered that she had not returned, that she was not here to help them, to tell them what to do next.

A great splashing from the bathroom; he ran back through the house, finding the boy out of the tub, crawling on his back like a crab, bouncing between the cabinets, the tub and toilet.

"Enough!" Benjamin tore the blanket from his bed and threw it over Cisco, the boy's body surging still, only gradually slowing, settling enough that Benjamin could gather him up—was he shivering?—and slide him into the bedroom, fight his sleepy resistance enough to dry him, to wrestle him onto the mattress. He leaned the boy to one side, folded the blankets back, then rolled him over, tucked him in with the comforter pulled up under his chin. Shadows still hovered above the skin of his face.

Cisco's breathing slowed. His forehead was cool, the room still.

The sound of the rain on the rooftop and, beyond it, something else. Something beneath the bed? Benjamin kneeled down, looked under.

No. Something in the basement.

Through the living room, into the kitchen, he switched on the light above the stairs.

Below, a shape leapt sideways, a clatter.

"Who's there?"

No answer.

Slowly, he began to descend. At the bottom of the stairs, he pulled on the hanging string and the light came on; he waited for his eyes to settle, all the tools reflecting from the wall. Nothing moved, yet there was a scuffle in the darkness, another sound. Breathing.

"Hello?" Benjamin said.

Hiding beneath the workbench, trembling, Johnson whined; the dog nervously licked his lips, growling and trying to get further back as Benjamin approached.

"Okay, then. You're fine, you're safe, boy."

As he ascended the stairs, Benjamin's feet made a squishy sound; he bent over to pull the Velcro loose on his sandals, then had to sit on the kitchen floor to struggle with his wet socks. The sound of rain, a cold wind blew through the house; the back door was still propped open.

Outside, it was dusk, darker than he expected. It was too dark to find anything inside the camper of Melissa's truck. Blindly, he opened cabinets and drawers until he found a box of matches, then a flashlight and, finally, what he sought—a bag of dog food. He rolled up the top and put the bag under his arm, climbed back down, locked the door behind him.

Back in the house, in the kitchen, he rattled some of the

kibble in a bowl, filled another with water. He made his way down the stairs and set them on the basement floor; slowly, cautiously—keeping his body low—Johnson crept forward. He fearfully glanced up the stairs, past Benjamin, and finally began to eat.

"You're safe."

Turning, he hurried back to the bedroom, where he found Cisco still sleeping, his eyes shut, blurred face restful, pale scratched hands like claws atop the blanket. He breathed deeply, almost gasping, then took several shallow breaths; the shadow over his face shifted, stretched and regathered with these changes, like fog above a lake.

"It's Johnson," Benjamin said, softly. "I think he's afraid of you, the way you are, now."

He stepped closer, sat on the bed; he swung his legs up, the cuffs of his pants wet from the bath, his feet bare; he leaned back against the headboard and closed his eyes.

Did he fall asleep?

Cisco stirred, kicked his legs. His mouth began to twist and tremble. Suddenly his tongue stuck out—eyes closed, shadows slipping—and then a clicking from his throat, and a voice:

"Cle, clev, cle, clever."

The raspy sound of the boy's breathing, and then his voice again, humming, and rapid syllables that made no sense together. Cisco kicked his legs, agitated, flailed his arms; the lamp on the bedside table rocked back and forth but did not tip over. His arms and legs were crawling at the ceiling, as if he were climbing an invisible ladder, still on his back.

"Meliss, Mel, Meliss. Wait."

The boy went silent. His breath came fast, a panting, limbs twitching, and only gradually slowed, everything settling, his breath still, silent, calm.

The rain on the rooftop.

A car drove by, outside, splashing through puddles.

As the room grew quiet again, as the house darkened, Benjamin closed his eyes. He lay one hand on Cisco's bare shoulder, resting it there, to reassure him, to not lose him.

Benjamin awakened alone on his bed, half sitting, his neck bent awkwardly. All the blankets were torn away, missing. The room smelled like a campfire—his tangle of clothes, still crumpled in the corner.

A creaking, another sound, somewhere in the house.

He stumbled, one leg still asleep. Through the doorway, into the living room, toward the kitchen.

The boy sat on the floor, illuminated by the light of the open refrigerator. A blanket around his shoulders as he took a bite from a stick of butter, a half loaf of bread resting in his lap. Benjamin approached, slowly; Cisco, startled, dropped the food, crawled sideways, all knees and elbows.

"What, you?" The boy didn't stand; the blanket had slipped away from him. His bristly red hair stuck up in every direction. "You're here . . . ? Where even is this?"

"I live here. It's my house." Benjamin held up his hands, his voice soft. "It's okay, everything's fine."

"Seriously?" Cisco leapt up, staggered to the window, looked out; as he spoke, he jerked his head to one side, then the other, as if this were the only way to see what was straight in front of him. "Okay, yes! That's your yard, I can tell . . . so this is your house." He sat on the floor again. "But what . . . what'd you do to me?"

"I found you, in Melissa's truck." Benjamin stepped around him, closed the refrigerator. "Where is she?"

"But I don't remember you being . . . being there at all . . ."

"Where?"

Cisco closed his eyes, wincing, slowly shaking his head. Tremors and shadows ran under and over his skin, skin so pale it had a blue tinge on his chest, freckles dark on his thin shoulders. He pulled himself upright, staggered, kicked a chair over so it bounced on the floor. His arms shot out and slapped back to his sides as he lurched around the table— his legs seemed heavy, ungainly, as if he were learning how to walk—and past Benjamin. He stopped at the framed photograph on the wall, staring at it sideways while facing into the kitchen.

"Who's this? They look . . . looking like it's a great great time."

"That's me," Benjamin said.

"You're the man?" Cisco said, tapping the glass above the photograph. "So, what, you're the father . . . and that's a daughter and you're the father? You are the father of the daughter and the daughter . . . the daughter your daughter?"

"Exactly," Benjamin said.

"So you had a daughter?"

"I still do."

Cisco laughed, a kind of giggle, the pitch of his voice shifting up, and with that there was a clatter on the stairs and Johnson shot forward, into the kitchen. He yelped, then collided into the boy as if he'd never expected to see him again. The two began wrestling happily across the floor, scattering paper, pushing furniture aside. Finally they tired, slowed.

"No one told . . . told me Johnson was here!" Cisco said, kissing the dog's head. "The best! But I'm hungry . . . I'm hungry . . . I'm freaking starving here, boss."

"Okay, yes. Wait. You must be cold, too. Wait here, just wait—"

He rushed to the bedroom, pulled clothes from the dresser and returned to the kitchen, set them on the floor next to Cisco. The boy was rubbing Johnson's belly.

Benjamin opened a cupboard, took out a pan, cracked two eggs into it, turned on the burner.

And then the boy was suddenly next to him, standing, striking Benjamin's shoulder with an open hand and shouting, the dog barking in reaction.

"Whoa, what? We're freaking twins!" Cisco now wore a white T-shirt, red suspenders, jeans with cuffs rolled high above his ankles. "Ha! These are totally . . . totally your clothes."

"Of course they are."

"It's hilarious, boss! We're hilarious."

Benjamin set down a plate of eggs and toast, and the boy dropped to his knees and crawled to the table, devoured them without standing or sitting in a chair, hardly using his fork. The haze over his face had thinned enough that his freckles showed through, and it also blended in with the bruises along his jaw and neck.

"More?" he said. "I'm starved . . . starving . . . so starved."

"Was Melissa with you?"

"Melissa?"

"When was the last time you saw her?"

"We built a fire," Cisco said. "We totally cooked this dough on branches on sticks . . . sticks . . . it was pretty epic! Then we made this fort thing . . . fort with sleeping bags and sleeping so I slept in there, and then I woke up and there I was . . . and they were telling me and they were telling me and then here here I was, eating breakfast, and then Johnson was here, too, and this is your house, and you had a daughter——"

"Who was telling you?"

"I'm starving!" He laughed the high-pitched laugh again. "Can you see me starving here?"

Benjamin set down another plate of food and Cisco sat in a chair, began eating more slowly. Next, a glass of milk; Benjamin helped him get a firm grasp on it, and Cisco drank, gulping, setting the empty glass down hard on the tabletop. He gasped, then burped.

"That boy! He told me told me. I mean, they were nice and everything . . . and everything, but that boy—his neck was totally . . . totally sliced! His head all fallen onto his back . . . like, backward, so his head was hanging there . . . and I had to walk around behind him to hear . . . him to hear what he was saying to me, which looked . . . looked totally weird because his mouth his mouth was upside upside down."

"This is the boy, the same boy from the house?"

"Now, what? Who?"

"The boy with the sister?"

Cisco suddenly leaned into the wall, then abruptly slid against it, all the way to the floor, collapsing, eyes closed. Johnson rushed out from under the kitchen table to lick his face; the shadows there swirled away and gathered again.

Benjamin knelt close. Cisco was breathing, his chest rising, falling. Resting. The street out the window, the rain still falling.

The boy trembled, then, his hands twitched, his bare feet slapping the floor, and he began crawling—crab-walking, collapsing and starting clumsily again. Benjamin bent over, stumbled, tried to guide him along the wall, to the bedroom doorway and through.

"The boy boy what?" Cisco said, his voice a shout that tapered away. His leg kicked up onto the bed and Benjamin managed to catch it, to hoist him, to roll him over, to get him back under the blankets.

Cisco's body shivered, trembled, finally settled; his ragged breathing eased and became regular, quiet, until there was only the sound of rain on the rooftop.

Benjamin sat next to the boy, his back against the head-board, his heart still so fast in his chest. Another sound—a scratching, footsteps—and then Johnson came through the door. The dog leapt up, circled several times at the foot of the bed, and collapsed with a sigh.

ONLY THE VOICES, rushing through the branches of hidden trees. Words broken up. He had no shadow, he could hardly feel the ground, no friction. A glowing, hazy landscape slipped around him. Only the voices through the branches of the trees.

Benjamin opened his eyes. Johnson was barking.

The dog, standing on the bed, suddenly leapt away, claws scrabbling from the bedroom, toward the front door.

Someone was knocking.

Cisco did not awaken, didn't stir. Benjamin pulled the blanket over the boy, then swung his feet to the floor. Stepping out of the bedroom, he closed the door behind him. He leaned close to the front window, peeked around the curtain, squinting against the gray light.

It was Helen, standing there waiting in the rain. A red knit cap on her head, a long coat.

Slowly, he turned the knob, eased the door open.

"Your face," she said, taking half a step back, almost tumbling down the steps.

"It's nothing." He touched the rough skin of his cheek, around his eye. "It's fine, now."

"What's going on with the dog?"

"Him?" Benjamin held Johnson—trying to lunge past—back with one leg. "I'm just watching him for someone—"

"Is he friendly?" she said. "Can I come in?"

Johnson snuffled at Helen's feet, at her hands; his wagging tail slapped the wall as she stepped inside, past Benjamin, toward the kitchen. Unbuttoning her coat, she looked over all the plates and pans on the counter, in the sink, the splatter of milk on the floor.

"The things you were saying, in the message," she said. "The lake, the dead children talking to you." She hung her coat over the back of a chair. "It was a lot. Let's not start with that, not right away."

"I didn't know you were coming," he said. "I mean, I'm glad."

"I tried to call. I sent a fax."

Across the room, he could see the white sheet of paper, a new message in the tray of the machine.

"It smells like smoke," she said, glancing out the window. "And whose truck is that, in the driveway?"

"Melissa's. My friend Melissa's."

"This is her dog?"

"Yes."

Johnson was whining, now, his snout pressed against the bottom of the closed bedroom door, his claws scratching the floor.

"She's here?" Helen said.

"Who?" he said. "No, no."

"Someone must be in there."

Stepping closer, he touched her shoulder, led her back through the living room.

"Something's happened," he said. "Something's happening."

A finger to his lips, he eased the bedroom door open. Helen leaned in, to see around him.

Gray light slanted through the window, onto the bed, where Cisco slept. The boy rested on his back, the dark haze shifting gently across his face; he twitched and the shadows jerked, settled.

"What happened to him?" Helen said, whispering. "Did you do this?"

"I found him."

"You found him?"

Johnson suddenly pushed past them; the dog stretched his snout toward Cisco, trying to lick the boy's face.

"This morning, in the truck," Benjamin said.

Helen turned away. He followed, into the kitchen, out of the room, the dog trailing them both.

"Well." She sat down at the table, her hands holding its edge. "You found a boy, this morning."

"But I know him—I mean, I already knew him. That's Cisco, Melissa's brother."

"Melissa," she said.

"He's resting." Benjamin pulled out a chair, but did not sit down. "He's getting better; I don't even think he has a fever anymore. He was talking, before, it seemed like he was getting better."

Helen took off her red cap, set it beside her on the table, then picked it up and put it on again.

"He went somewhere with Melissa, and he got lost," Benjamin said. "What he said was kind of hard to follow, the way he was talking."

"And what about Melissa? Where's she?"

"I don't know."

"Can you call her?"

"Not really," he said. "No. She'll be back soon, I think. She'll know what to do."

Helen glanced toward the bedroom, then looked at Benjamin again. She closed her eyes, slowly opened them.

"Have you told anyone?"

"Who would I tell?"

"I don't know," she said. "His parents?"

"I don't think he has parents."

"Somewhere, he does."

And then a kind of shout, a crash. They both rushed back into the bedroom, the dog's barking echoing everywhere around them.

Cisco had fallen between the bed and the wall and was kicking, hands climbing and crawling, rattling in that space until they pulled him back onto the bed, slowed his arms and legs.

He panted, his mouth open, tongue sticking out, hands clenched tight. His eyes blinked rapidly, blinked and blinked, the dark irises jerking to the outside edges. At last, his breathing eased; he seemed about to fall asleep, then— eyes wide and white—slowly turned his head back and forth, as if scanning Helen's face.

"Hello," he said.

"Hello."

"Who? You are who?"

"I'm Helen."

"Do I know you?"

"No."

"I do, I do. I like like you. I like her."

"She's my daughter," Benjamin said.

"From the from the picture. All grown grown up!"

"What?" Helen said.

"The photograph," Benjamin said. "In the other room."

"Seems like——" Cisco stood without warning, laughing his high-pitched laugh, and brushed past them, stumbling toward the living room; Johnson, excited, leapt beside him. "Seems like we have . . . have to we have to go, to get going."

"Wait," Benjamin said, following, Helen close behind him.

In the living room, Cisco collapsed to the floor, flipped onto his back and crawled that way, his clouded face toward the ceiling, looking back at them; next, he pulled himself upright, unsteady, took two steps and collapsed again. He crawled, he stood up and straightened himself; his movements were jerky, almost mechanical.

"Cisco," Benjamin said.

As the boy fell, then crawled, Helen stood to one side, her eyes fixed on him. Her feet set wide, her hands out from her sides, fingers spread. She stared at Cisco, her face trembling; it was as if Benjamin were not in the room at all.

Cisco, reaching the kitchen, began eating scraps from the counter, licking his fingers. He found an apple, took a bite, chewing as he switched his head from side to side, trying to see in every direction.

"You need to rest," Benjamin said. "We can help you."

"No . . . no, not. Not you help me. They told me!"

"Who told you?"

"The boy! The boy, the brother of the sister sister. I was

scared! I was like . . . what . . . the girl's skin was like falling off her face or something . . . or something and the boy was way worse. . . . They said, they said I'm supposed to help help you. And now, the snow! We have to go!"

"Wait."

"There's no waiting waiting but going." Cisco stumbled as he clattered to the back door, jerked it open. "What? Melissa's truck's here? She said . . . she told me it was broken? And we need to go, to go—"

"Where's Melissa?"

"We'll find out," Cisco said, "once we get there. I can't can't explain to you all the things . . . the things I can't explain I need to show you."

"Melissa will look for us, here," Benjamin said. "She'll know where to find us."

"It's not a choice of a thing." The boy stepped so close that Benjamin could feel the breath behind his words. "I need to show you . . . to go there to show you."

"Cisco," Benjamin said.

"You!" Cisco stepped toward Helen. "Help me help me help him."

"I don't know," she said.

"You do know. You know." He leaned closer, his face looking away, to see her. "I can tell! I feel how you felt and you felt how I feel—"

Helen crossed the room and opened the front door without a word. She went out, closed it behind her.

"It's not a choice of a thing!" Cisco was shouting, and already Benjamin was out the door, after her.

Rain slashed across the gray sky. Closer to her rental car, Benjamin could see that Helen was just sitting there, in the passenger seat. Her face rested in her hands; she rubbed at her eyes. He took another step closer, the wet concrete cold beneath his bare feet, the rain on his head.

She looked up and saw him, before he reached the car. She rolled the window down.

"Are you leaving?" he said.

"I just needed a minute." Helen was looking past him, at the house. "I don't think I can leave, now."

Cisco—in the baggy jeans and white T-shirt, the red suspenders—was waving from the porch, the dog leaping excitedly beside him. Hands around his mouth, he shouted:

"We need to get ready! To prepare, to make preparations! It's freaking freaking cold—"

Half an hour later, they pulled away from the house—
Helen driving, Cisco in the passenger seat, Benjamin and
Johnson in back.

"The snow!" Shadows swirled across the boy's face, his
eyes white, irises wide. "Up by the mountains and everything and the snow and the snow."

"Left, here," Benjamin said.

They took the side streets, puddles everywhere,
driving past where the children's house had been. The
freshly poured foundation glowed pale gray against the
rain.

"We," Cisco said, "we brought food?"

"We packed it all up, remember? And the clothes, there
in the bag by your feet."

"These clothes." Cisco leaned forward and dug through

them, pulling out an orange balaclava. "What where . . . we're looking freaking freaking ridiculous."

"Just so they're warm enough."

"People are going to say—" Cisco's voice wavered, quieter. "What'll they say?"

"What people?"

The boy was already asleep.

. . .

THE RAIN THICKENED to sleet as they passed the outskirts of Gresham and drove through Boring, out onto Highway 26. Cisco, still asleep, slumped over, his head almost in Helen's lap as she drove.

"We'll just see what he wants to show us," Benjamin said. "Are you doing okay?"

Helen rolled down her window, the cold blustery rush around them all at once; she stuck her bare hand outside then pulled it in, pressed it against the skin of her face. When she spoke it was not to Benjamin, her voice so soft he could barely hear it:

"I felt how you feel and you feel how I felt."

She rolled up the window, changed lanes. They passed a school bus, the bleary faces of children above looking out, sliding away.

"Is this too much?" Benjamin said. "Everything—"

Helen reached her right hand back between the seats; he reached out to hold it in his own.

"It's all right," she said, squeezing his fingers, not pulling away. "It's a lot, but it feels familiar, too—it's a relief, somehow. We'll just see what we see."

. . .

TEN MINUTES LATER, Cisco pulled himself upright, checked Benjamin and Johnson in the back. The boy's face was clearer, now; it looked smudged, dirty, his freckles showing through. His irises pulled into the middle of his eyes for a moment, then jerked wide again.

"How you feeling?" Helen said.

Cisco switched on the radio, spun the dial to static; he swiveled his head from side to side, his red cowlicks seeming to tremble in resonance with the sound.

"We didn't forget the food?" he said.

"We have the food," she said.

Cisco leaned forward, found the pack that held the groceries, pulled it onto his lap, rustled through it. Setting a piece of bread on each knee, he began constructing a peanut butter and jelly sandwich. Johnson stretched his neck between the front seats, watching.

"Wait," Helen said, glancing at Benjamin. "I just realized— is this the same dog that bit you? Your face?"

Cisco slapped the two pieces of bread together, held it out so Johnson could snatch it, and began making a new sandwich.

"That was a long time ago," Benjamin said.

Outside, the snow fell in heavy flakes, the wipers struggling to keep up. A sign for chains and traction tires blinked, loomed ahead, was swallowed away behind them. A truck passed, kicking up slush, blinding them for a moment, and then the highway reappeared, two black lines in all the white. Skibowl flashed by on the right, then the town of Government Camp on the left. Benjamin watched the edge of Helen's face. Her ear, sticking out below the red cap. Her smooth jawline tense, pulsing.

"Here!" Cisco said. "Go up there!"

They climbed the road toward Timberline Lodge. All the blacktop under the snow, white, the snow still falling. Drifts rose higher than the car's roof on each side, the road a bright winding tunnel. After about a mile, they came around a bend and there—to the left, on the downhill side—was a break in the wall of snow, a ragged edge with yellow plastic tape stretched across it.

"There," Cisco said.

"Nowhere to park," Helen said.

Fifty yards later, she pulled over in a chain-up area.

"The dog?" Benjamin said.

"Let's leave him here."

Cisco was already outside, wrapping a rainbow-colored scarf around his neck, zipping up a puffy blue down jacket patched with duct tape. Finally he pulled on the knit orange balaclava and began running awkwardly ahead, feet sliding on the ice, his huge mittened hands, also orange, out wide.

Helen helped Benjamin into his red coat, then held his arm as they carefully crossed the road, along the slippery shoulder. Behind them, Johnson's muffled barking, the car's windows fogged up.

A truck veered around them, heading downhill. Someone shouted out the window; Cisco slowed, began to shout a reply and fell over onto his side, his limbs a tangle, flailing and kicking and then crawling—he zigzagged, skittered like a crab down the shoulder of the road, disappearing under the yellow plastic tape, off the road, beyond where they could see.

Benjamin and Helen hurried after him, leaning together, to the place where the snowdrift was broken. Thin red fiberglass rods jutted out, here and there, the yellow tape stretched between them. They crawled over the tape, on all fours, approaching Cisco; he was facing away, on his stomach, looking over the edge.

"Damn, boss," the boy said, turning his head from side to side to see straight. "Your car is so over!"

At the bottom of the steep slope, at the end of a long scar of dirt and rocks and uprooted trees, rested Benjamin's Subaru. It was upside down, the tatters of its black tires in the air, its roof flattened beneath it. Snow swirled around in the space between the car and where they were crouched.

"Melissa," Benjamin said.

"They told me about this! Where I was!" Cisco shouted above the wind. "She's here! I mean, her body's right down there, under the snow . . . under the snow, but if the dogs couldn't find it didn't find it, no way we're finding finding it. What would we even do if we did find it?" He held up his mittened hands. "Melissa's all sorts of places, now. She's not coming not coming back here, never not never coming back. Even if she wanted if she wanted to come back, she couldn't, and she doesn't even want to."

Wind swept the snow through the air, the snow making the wind visible.

"Up we go!" Cisco slid down to the road, then stumbled to his feet, headed toward the car.

At Timberline, a few RVs were parked at one end of the lot, cars scattered here and there, rooftops capped with snow. Despite the storm, it was still early November, and the lifts weren't yet open. Lights shone in the hooded windows of the lodge, which stood, all dark wood and shingles, hulking against the whiteness.

Cisco opened the passenger door while the car was still moving; he stuck his foot outside, the skittery sound of his boot sliding on the ice.

"Hold on," Benjamin said. "What—"

"This, boss. It's not a thing like that, with a choice I'm choosing. I know. I need to show you."

The car came to a stop and Cisco leapt out and raced away, snow whipping around him; he ran bent over, caught between staying on his feet or going down on all fours.

Halfway across the parking lot, he checked, then rushed back to be sure they were following. He waved his mittened hands, shouting something they couldn't hear; with the balaclava pulled down to cover his face, he looked like a yarn puppet with human lips and those white eyes.

"Okay," Helen said. "Let's see what he wants to show us, then?"

Johnson barked and whined, trying to climb between the seats. Benjamin struggled to attach the leash to the dog, then opened the door and was jerked outside, almost pulled off his feet.

The slick ground, the cold, the sharp wind everywhere. As he steadied himself against the hood of the car, he could see Helen, inside: her hands still on the wheel, her eyes closed, her lips moving as if she was talking to herself. And then her eyes opened. She climbed out, looked across at him and zipped her coat up high, the fur hood closed tight around her face. When she locked the car, the horn beeped once, the sound absorbed almost immediately by the snow-banks around them.

"Hurry!" Cisco leapt ahead, crookedly across the parking lot, up a drift pockmarked with footprints.

Helen helped Benjamin climb. In the open, the wind came sharp and cold, the snow still falling. Above, on the slope, chairs hung empty, swinging like dark cages from their cables.

"Look at this!" Cisco was saying as he stamped on the ground, atop a straight dark piece of wood. "This is the top of a sign! Here, let Johnson loose—he can totally help us find . . . find the way."

Johnson bounded ahead, black against the white, Cisco behind him.

"Epic!" he called back. "It's not so far, now. Not far at all! I can feel it I can feel how to go already. I feel really good, now."

Johnson doubled back to check on them, his muzzle white with frost, then lunged ahead. They walked through a stand of trees, sheltered from the wind, then out in the open again. Benjamin felt the frames of his eyeglasses, frozen and brittle against his face, the hairs sharp in his nose. Behind him, below, he could not see the parking lot, the lodge.

"Dad?" Helen said. "You okay?"

"Fine."

Ahead then—a figure—two figures—moving toward them.

Disappearing in the whiteness, appearing again, closer, weaving and sliding, coming together.

"Here they come," Benjamin said.

"Who?" she said.

Yet it was actually only one person, on skis, spraying snow as Johnson barked, as the figure came to a stop. It was a man, snowshoes strapped to his back. Frost in his beard, goggles over his eyes.

"What are you thinking?" he said, gasping for breath. "Storm coming in, it's getting dark. You're heading in the wrong direction!"

"We're good," Cisco said, jerking his head from side to side to look at the skier. "It's just a little little further."

The man looked them over, leaning on his poles. "A little further to where?"

"We're fine," Helen said. "We'll turn back soon."

"Okay, suit yourselves then." The man pulled his goggles back down, pushed off, and slid away, behind them, gone into the whiteness.

They stood still for a moment in the silence.

"Real, real close," Cisco said. "Come on, Johnson."

"Here," Helen said to Benjamin, "you go in front of me, so I can see you."

They climbed until they were above the tree line. Snow came sideways, then seemed to be falling upward from the ground, white in every direction.

"Hold on to me," Cisco said, the loose end of the dog's makeshift leash in his mittened hand. He'd tied the other end around his waist, and now twisted the balaclava so his eyes were covered, so the eyeholes faced back, tufts of hair sticking out; he led them upward, stumbling blind, foundering in the snow and finding his way.

They kept on. Benjamin couldn't feel his toes, his feet; it was as if he were walking on his ankles, balancing, falling forward again and again. The wind buffeted them, drove the flakes along the surface of the mountain, whistled, its tone rising and falling.

Ahead, Helen pointed out a flicker, something blue, shining amid all the white. Closer, it winked away, then reappeared.

"Oho!" Cisco spun the balaclava around again, his eyes suddenly staring from its holes, his teeth showing as he smiled. "There you are!"

Half buried in the snow, dug into the slope, stood the lean-to; its blue tarp slanted down, a frosty woolen blanket hung across to cover the opening.

"Hello!" Cisco knelt down. "Anyone in there?"

The wind hissed around them.

"Hurry," Helen said. "We'll freeze out here."

Crawling in, they elbowed and kicked each other in the darkness, Johnson whining, licking at their faces as they unwrapped their scarves. Benjamin found a flashlight, a headlamp, and then the battery-powered lantern.

"Everything's here," he said. "Blow up the sleeping pads, so we have some insulation, something to sit on."

The snow beneath them was packed hard, as if someone had been here before, and it radiated cold into the bones of his knees. He found the stove, the can of fuel and, with Helen's help, began boiling a pot of water.

. . .

BEFORE LONG THEY were huddled together, inside sleeping bags, blankets on top of them, drinking hot chocolate and eating bowls of ramen as the wind whistled and howled outside, as ropes and straps slapped the tarp overhead.

Johnson sniffed for the crumbs of the kibble they'd brought along, that he'd already eaten. Cisco pushed his balaclava up so it sat like another sagging face atop his head.

"I'm afraid," the boy said, his voice soft. "I'm actually a little afraid, now. Aren't you afraid?"

"Yes," Helen said. "I am afraid, but we're afraid together."

"What," Cisco said. "I know you, I know I know you, but what is your name again?"

"Helen."

"Helen," the boy said. "You know what what's going to happen?"

"No," she said. "We'll wait out the storm, is one thing."

A blast of icy snow sifted in; Benjamin reached out, held down the edge of the blanket.

"I'm so tired," Cisco said, "and I'm afraid afraid to sleep because this is as far as I know . . . I'm afraid to . . . sleep to fall asleep."

"That you'll wake up and things will be different?" Benjamin said.

"That's what always happens, seems like." The boy reached out, scratched Johnson's head. "Every morning seems different. But you . . . you're not afraid to sleep?"

"Here," Helen said to Cisco, spreading the mats along the snow-packed floor. "I'll stay with you. I'm right here. If you do fall asleep, wherever you wake up, I'll be there, too. And when the storm passes, we'll walk down to the car."

"You can't promise that," Cisco said.

"I can. I will. You can tie that leash to your wrist, and to mine. Here."

. . .

THE RUSH AND hiss, the bluish light flashing in the gap between the tarp and the blanket. Benjamin closed his eyes. He was stretched out closest to the door, Johnson nestled against him, the dog's rank breath in his face. On the other side of Johnson was Helen, and then Cisco. The space inside the lean-to was like an igloo, warmed by their bodies, insulated by the snow.

"I can't sleep," Cisco said, his voice faint against the wind.

"Just rest," Helen said. "We have to wait. It'll go faster if you sleep."

"I'm afraid."

The tarp above shook and crackled, as if hands were slapping from outside. Cold air knifed in.

"When I was a girl," Helen said, "even younger than you, I had a brother, a little brother——"

"I know that," Cisco said. "That's the one you went look looking for."

"His name was Derek," she said, "and I could hear him at night, crying in his room, because sometimes he was afraid to fall asleep."

"You were trying to find him to find him."

"And I'd slip out of my bed and crawl down the hallway, past my parents' room—the floor creaked, on one side, so I pressed myself against the other wall, and I opened his door so slowly, so it would stay quiet. He watched from his crib, through the wooden bars, and then I crawled right under, beneath him, the metal springs and the mattress between us. He could hear me breathing, and I could hear him, and then he'd be able to fall asleep."

THE FRANTIC SLAPPING of the blue tarp where a corner was loose, the wind ripping across the frozen mountainside.

Benjamin opened his eyes, rolled over. He found his glasses, zipped away in a pocket of the sleeping bag, and put them on.

There—Helen's pale face, asleep with the cap on her head, the blankets pulled up to her chin. And now he felt the warm shape of Johnson, the dog all the way under the sleeping bags and blankets. Cisco, too, more difficult to see, only the top of his head visible, the balaclava dark against the white snow of the floor.

Stretching out his hand, Benjamin touched the wool blanket that hung across the doorway; its edges frosty, stiff against his fingers. He pulled his hand back into the warmth of his sleeping bag and slept once more.

THIS TIME, HE awakened to silence. No wind.

The ground surrounding the pile of sleeping bags and blankets was covered in green moss, not white snow.

He sat up, his head almost pressing against the blue tarp.

"Helen?

"Cisco?

"Johnson?"

He kicked his legs wide and did not feel the dog. The other sleeping bags lay flat, empty. He reached out, the wool blanket no longer frosty, and pulled it aside.

Daylight flooded into the lean-to. Here, their bowls and mugs, the empty hot chocolate packets, the stove and fuel container.

Outside, tall trees against the pale sky, no snow, no steep incline. A meadow, stumps, and fifty feet away, the smooth waters of the lake.

He swung his legs around, dug through the blankets until he found one boot, then the other, and forced his feet inside. Crawling out feetfirst, he pulled himself upright. The sky glowed, the sun behind the clouds. He tried to jump, his boots just lifting from the frozen ground, and settled, pain in his knees.

"Helen?" he called. "Helen? Cisco?"

Birds answered at the sound of his voice, but he could not see them. Snow shone white in the shadows beneath the trees.

"Johnson?"

Not even the dog could hear him.

He walked, red shoelaces trailing, to the edge of the lake. The water stretched away, clear and dark, the sharp white bones against the darker lake bed.

Would the children show themselves, surface again? He squinted into the depths.

A darker edge, among the deep shadows, the water thick

and bending, a current, a straight edge with blacker darkness on one side. A kind of door?

A shape flashed, pale against the blackness. A fish, fluttering at the edge of the doorway. Or a hand, at the end of an arm, beckoning, gesturing for him to descend.

And he was already stepping in, the cold sharp through his boots, his socks, up over his ankles, his calves, his knees. The underwater rocks slippery beneath his feet, he waded in. Thighs, waist, stomach, chest. His clothes floated lightly, both on and merely hovering around his body.

The trees seemed to bend in, over the lake, as he went deeper. He heard the birds calling, yet still saw no birds against the pale sky.

He held his glasses to his face as the cold water climbed up his neck, over his mouth, his nose, and then the sound shifted, his ears full of cold, thick water, and what he saw were white bones around him, and fish—trout, sharp and startled, bending to look back at him, to check, to believe what they were seeing.

The water went red, solid red, and he realized that it was his coat, rising to float around him. He raised one arm and the sleeve pulled itself inside out, the current taking hold; he lifted his other arm and the whole coat pulled away, sailing slowly free, scattering fish.

Next, his down vest, his shirt. He kicked off one boot, then the other, unbuttoned his pants.

His clothing floated away, unfurling so fluidly, like a ghost torn to pieces. In stockinged feet and eyeglasses, he descended.

The lake's flat surface, his ceiling, glowed above and behind him, holding the bent shadows of trees; beneath him, the door. Not open, but ajar, with no handle or doorknob, no hand beckoning him.

He could only move so fast, his approach gradual, incremental.

A cloud passed over, blocking the light—no, it was only his coat again, spinning fluidly overhead. Now a sound, a sound like dogs barking, underwater, heavy and slow and elongated, echoing.

Another dark shadow, higher, above the surface sliding along and then crashing through—a splash, a white commotion of bubbles, dark sticks resolving into legs, a dark body, and then Johnson's snout, the dog sinking to the shallows, stumbling along the lake bed, down the slope to the depths, toward Benjamin.

The dog half swam, half ran, his body switching back and forth, back legs out above and behind him. He floated backward, he lunged forward, downward, making slow progress.

Benjamin waited, watched, looking up through the

water, to the surface where the tall pines leaned, their sharp points tilting in.

His vision stretched, it rose and rose, up out of the water and into the trees; he seemed to float above them, wheeling until he was looking straight down—as if he were suspended in the air above the trees, and now the scene had changed: the trees were surrounded by snow, they did not circle a lake, and on the steep slope, a square of blue, the wind burying the roof of the lean-to.

And, closer, he could see the wool blanket shiver, ice breaking free as it shifted to one side, and then a flash of orange—Cisco, crawling out, and, behind him, Helen. They stood, then began untying the leash that connected them, the knots at their wrists.

"Where did that dog go?" Helen said.

"With him, I guess," Cisco said.

"What?"

"That's not even him, in there."

Turning, Cisco pulled the wool blanket up, flipped it aside.

Still in its sleeping bag, Benjamin's body rested, the skin of his face grayish blue, the light through the tarp above, and his eyes open, staring and staring, seeing nothing.

"That's just his body," Cisco said. "He's somewhere else. He's not here, you can tell."

Helen didn't say anything; stepping close, she knelt down, reached out and touched Benjamin's face—did he feel it?—then gently pulled the wool blanket across again.

"He's somewhere else," Cisco said, again.

They started down the slope, the wind still howling, the snow filling in the footprints behind them and drifting around the lean-to, the blue tarp, beginning to cover it all. Helen looked back, once, and before long they had zig-zagged out of sight, into the trees.

Benjamin, standing at the bottom of the lake, watched them go. And just as they slipped beneath the trees, beyond where he could see, he felt something against his leg— Johnson, the dog brushing past him, through the door. Benjamin reached out to pat him, the dog's body strangely buoyant, giving way. He tried to take hold of Johnson's tail, but he was too slow.

Grasping the edge of the door, he pulled it open further, his body floating around into the opening.

The thin quickness of air on his hands, his chest, his face, a brightness that blinded him. The ground was smooth, soft beneath his stockinged feet; the socks were all he wore, and yet he was not cold.

The air glowed, dense with fog, he had no shadow, there was no sign of the sun.

The thick smell of sage, of pine.

Ahead, beyond him, voices called. Words broken up, or in a language he could not quite understand. Familiar, welcoming voices, at different volumes, from various distances and times: the brother and sister from the murder house, and Melissa, and—further away, words torn and buffeted—even his son, Derek, whose small voice he had never forgotten.

There was no door, now, no walls, no sky, no ground. No feet, no legs, no arms, no hands. Only the voices, rushing through the branches of hidden trees.